INSTANT REPLAY

MARA JACOBS

Copper Country Press LLC

ISBN: 978-1-940993-19-5

O h my God, it's nothing but naked men in here!" Marlee said on a bit of a squeak. Which was unusual, because calm, cool Marlee Reeves never squeaked.

"Where? Where?" Marlee's friend, Kathy Robinson, peeked around Marlee's tall shoulder, looking past the foyer where they stood, and down into the sunken living room.

"Everywhere. There, and there." Marlee pointed out the men in question to Kathy.

"Marlee, if that's your idea of naked men, you've been in the classroom way too long." Kathy chuckled and shook her head at Marlee.

Kathy was one of the few people Marlee knew who didn't think of her as uptight, because Kathy had seen her when Marlee let her hair down, both figuratively and literally, when they'd been roommates at Berkeley. But most people when meeting Marlee—for the first, second, and even third times— came away thinking of a stereotypical cool, buttoned-up priss. And that was fine with her.

She supposed it didn't help that she perpetuated the

stereotype by wearing nothing but severely cut business suits, her auburn hair always bound up in a tight chignon, and the requisite glasses. The suits were designer, as were the glasses, and very fashionable, but still.

Kathy had told her to dress casually for the football game they'd gone to earlier that day, and she had…or so she'd thought. Kathy, upon seeing her, had laughed and asked her if she even owned jeans. Marlee had only smiled and told her friend that she would be fine in what she was wearing.

And Kathy hadn't said a word at the looks Marlee received as they'd walked through the crowd at Liberty Field to watch the Pumas lose to the Jets, taking them out of the playoffs and ending their season. Amidst the face-painted, bare beer-bellied Pumas diehards sat Marlee, in a gray Donna Karan paint suit with cream silk blouse underneath, all covered by a camel hair coat and cashmere scarf.

A large whoop from the crowd in the living room in front of them brought Marlee back from her musings on her wardrobe, and she once again concentrated on the wardrobes of the people in front of her.

Or, rather, lack of wardrobes.

"Semi-naked, then," Marlee amended. It was still an awful lot of flesh. It was wall-to-wall bodies, mostly female. Kathy and she were descending into the living room of the home, had just passed the foyer, when the visual Technicolor of the outfits and the overwhelming aroma of nearly fifty different designer perfumes assaulted Marlee's senses.

There were probably thirty men. They were all huge. A true rainbow coalition. The skin tones ran the gamut from palest white to blackest black, with every hue in between represented. Marlee assumed that these men were the players she had watched earlier today.

Tried to watch. The game moved faster than she'd

imagined. She'd left the game with a headache, hoping for a quiet dinner with her friend Kathy and her husband Joey. This loud, body-filled house was not what she had in mind.

The men at the party all wore either muscle shirts or no shirt at all, and nylon running pants. Maybe regular pants just wouldn't fit over thighs like theirs, though it seemed to Marlee that surely these men's salaries would allow them some custom tailoring. The huge biceps on most of them would cut glass, they were so hard. That must be the reason for the sleeveless shirts—to show off the bulging muscles. It certainly wasn't to stay cool. Not in January in Boston. Marlee looked, but was hard-pressed to find a neck on any of them. It seemed their burly chests blended right into their massive heads.

The women were just as scantily dressed. Halter tops, tank tops, and even a sprinkling of tube tops. Lots of them in lamé. All worn a size too small. In the dead of a Boston winter. Marlee shivered just thinking of how cold the women must be. They didn't act cold, though, unless their close proximity to all the men in the room was an effort to bask in the collective body heat. Marlee wasn't sure which was more plentiful at first glance: big hair or nearly bared breasts.

Marlee hadn't seen so much cleavage since the time she had inadvertently gone to a strip joint with some male colleagues after a conference, thinking that "The Trim Club" was a new workout place.

Kathy had taken her to the football game—Marlee's first—and now they were at an after-game party at a home belonging to one of the players. Marlee and Kathy were there to collect Kathy's husband Joey, who was a former teammate of the man who was hosting the party.

Joey played for the Portland Lumberjacks, and their season had ended a week earlier. He'd wanted to come to a game of a former teammate of his who was retiring. As it happened, with the loss today, it turned out to be his final game.

Marlee didn't care about any of that, but she was thrilled to see her old roommate Kathy and meet her husband. When they'd married so quickly after meeting last year, Marlee had been concerned. But even just spending this short amount of time with them, she could see the couple was deeply in love.

But now, Marlee just wanted to collect Joey and go to dinner. The thought of spending any more time in this place made her extremely uneasy. She felt like she did in high school when the football team strolled down the hall, slamming the nerdy boys into lockers, and the cheerleaders trailed after them, all twittering and giggling. It made her feel insignificant and out of place, even a little nervous. Those nerdy boys had been her friends, her fellow chess club members. And she had never had anything in common with the cheerleaders.

As she looked around the room, she pushed her glasses up her nose (a testament that she hadn't left her nerd roots totally behind). She wasn't sure if it was the huge men or the scantily clothed women that bothered her, but this was not her cup of tea. Nevertheless, she held herself with her usual poise and dignity, as if large men tossing a tiny woman above their heads and passing her across the room was an everyday occurrence.

She turned her attention away from the people and to the décor of the room. It was lovely. Marlee had assumed that they'd be going to an ostentatious mansion furnished in lots of black leather and chrome with big-screen TVs, quadraphonic stereo systems, and trophies lining every available inch of wall space. Possibly some zebra-skin rugs. But this place was no mansion, though it was definitely an expensive home.

The room they were in was what Marlee assumed was the great room. Through the throng of people she could see one wall was dominated by a gorgeous stone fireplace. Another wall was painted a Tuscan gold that set it apart from the rest of the room.

She'd done something similar in her home, painting one wall a dramatic salmon color. This player's wife and Marlee had similar tastes, and she debated trying to stay at the party long enough to meet the woman and to see the kitchen. She was a kitchen connoisseur.

The house was in the quiet, family-oriented, affluent Boston suburb of Brookline, one that Marlee had driven through many times, mentally adding it to her list of places she would look into when she settled down and had a family.

She wondered now, as she looked around the warm, homey decor, if she wouldn't be better off spending more time trying to find someone to share a home like this with than looking at neighborhoods.

"Look at all those glorious bare chests, all those muscles. Man, these guys are sculpted. Of course, none can hold a candle to my Joey. We better find him and get the heck out of here; looks like this place is about to get out of hand. I'm thinking this party is for the single players. I don't see too many wife-looking women here. Besides, I don't want him comparing me with all those nubile young groupies."

Kathy joked about her husband of just over a year, but Marlee knew that they were deliriously happy together. Joey's grandmother was staying with their baby in Portland while the couple took the quick trip to Boston so Joey could wish his friend well.

Joey had felt he should at least make an appearance at his friend's party, so he went right after the game, and Kathy and Marlee were to pick him up and the three would go out for dinner. Marlee had something she wanted to discuss with Joey, and she didn't want to do it with Metallica blasting in the background and young girls in spandex giggling in her ears.

As if Marlee had conjured him up, Joey stepped forward from the crowd and started walking toward them. He walked quickly, making several moves worthy of his football god status—just to avoid making contact with the huge men who were in various stages of dancing, drinking, flirting with the groupies, and lamenting the loss that had ended their season.

Joey wasn't alone. Beside him walked the most handsome man Marlee had ever seen. He was smaller than Joey, and was dwarfed by the behemoth football players who seemed to part like the Red Sea to allow the men past. He was dressed more like Joey too, in khakis, a crisp white dress shirt with its sleeves rolled up his tanned forearms, and very expensive loafers. Marlee, a shoe freak from way back, noticed the loafers first, made a note of the designer and the probable cost, and wondered if this man with Joey might be a team member's agent.

Marlee's chest tightened just from looking at the man coming their way. God, he was handsome. A physique to die for. He must work out a lot. If he was an agent, he had players for clients and maybe wanted to look good when he was next to them. And boy did he look good.

It was his size that was most attractive to Marlee. Big, strong, broad shoulders, but not hulking, overbearing strength, no oversized neck like the other men here had. This man was in perfect proportion. Deep brown hair and green eyes, a combination that Marlee always particularly liked. Being nearly five feet, ten inches herself, she was drawn to tall men. Not enough that she had to strain her neck to look up at them, but if her estimation was close, his six-foot frame would be perfect for her.

Perfect for her.

The idea breezed through Marlee's brain. Gorgeous, good dresser, most likely an agent or somebody in the Pumas' front office, so good employment and would be staying in the area. She stole a glance at his hand to see an absence of any wedding ring.

The night was looking up. The thought of staying at this party just got a whole lot more desirable. She could get to know this man and maybe get to see the kitchen as well. She could avoid meeting any of the football players by having Kathy, Joey, and this other man to talk to.

She didn't delude herself into thinking that any of the players would be falling all over themselves to meet her when there were so many other flashier, younger, and obviously more eager women in the room.

"Marlee Reeves, Declan Tate. Declan, Marlee. And this," he said, while swinging a large arm around tiny Kathy's shoulders, "is my sweet Kathy. Declan's bored here so he's going to join us for dinner, if that's okay with you ladies?"

"Okay? Okay? Of course it's okay. God, it's great to meet you," Kathy said as she shook Declan's hand. Marlee thought she was going a little overboard. Yes, the man was good looking, but Kathy had seen handsome men before—was married to one!—and had never gushed like this.

"Mr. Tate, nice to meet you." Marlee held her hand out to Declan. He took it, and piercing green eyes met Marlee's as he held her hand. His hand was rough and warm on her soft and cold one. She had not fully warmed up from being outside for the game, even though she'd had the car's heater at full blast on the ride over. Her palm, and then fingers, rapidly warmed as Declan held them.

Everything seemed to slow down to Marlee. The sounds from the party—which before had been grating—dulled, so that she could almost hear her heart beating. Faster. The perfume that had pervaded the air was now drowned out by the subtle hint of musk that emanated from the man still holding her hand.

"Please, call me Declan, Mrs. Reeves," he said.

Marlee would later try to analyze the waves of feelings she had as Declan held her hand. Exhilaration, excitement, definite attraction, but mainly confusion at the onslaught of emotions from simply shaking the man's hand.

Marlee was a respected professional. But she was also a woman, and emotion—more succinctly, lust—was overriding any logical thought that tried to occupy her brain.

THUNDERBOLT. THAT WAS HOW DECLAN DESCRIBED IT. Plain, old-fashioned thunderbolt.

And just what he needed tonight.

He'd been feeling out of sorts. These parties were not his usual after-game ritual, but this one was unavoidable. All he'd wanted to do tonight was soak in his hot tub, have a glass of wine—his first in months—and sulk. Well, maybe not sulk. Reflect…yeah, he wanted to reflect.

Reflect on his life, his past, and, more important, his future. He'd wanted to be alone, to let emotions pour over him unnoticed, to let the weariness of the last sixteen years finally rest on his shoulders.

To admit his life, as he had known it, was over.

That had been his plan. But here he was surrounded by men and women. Some, like his former teammate Joey Robinson, he'd known for years, some for only six months. Some he didn't know at all. He thought the party might get him out of his funk, but it had just drawn him in deeper.

Until he'd seen her. The most conspicuous person in the room, if only because she had the most clothes on.

He'd seen her come in as he'd watched from across the

room. He assumed one of the women was Joey's wife, because they certainly didn't look like all the other women who came to the after-game parties. For one thing, they were older. Not old, probably only thirty—which was still considered young to thirty-nine-year-old Declan—but still much older than every other female there.

They were dressed much more conservatively than the rest, as well. The one Declan had hoped was Joey's Kathy was in jeans and a Pumas jersey. She was the shorter of the two, maybe five-four, cute as a button with long hair and a fresh-faced good-girl look. Her slight frame was dwarfed by the jersey.

The other one, the one Declan hoped was not Joey's wife, meaning she might be unattached, sported a look that had never crossed the threshold of this house. And Declan liked it. He liked it a lot. He could honestly say he found himself drawn to it. Drawn to her.

Business suit, glasses, and a bun. She was beautiful. No makeup. Surely the only woman in the room, other than Kathy, to have on at least two layers. A perfectly formed oval face, with cheekbones that seemed even more pronounced due to her glasses. Declan glanced around and wondered how many people in this packed room, male and female, wore contacts and would rather die than be seen in glasses. Probably more than half. She was definitely refreshing. Just then she pushed the glasses up higher on her nose and the movement seemed almost alluring to Declan.

He couldn't tell much about her figure through the severely cut suit, but she was tall and nicely shaped from what he could see. He'd sure like to get that jacket off of her. Maybe she wasn't wearing anything under that cream blouse. Was it real silk? What would it feel like under his hands to unbutton it? Would it slip out of his grasp, take him several attempts to bare her skin? Declan wondered how sheer it was, if he'd be able to see the outline of a camisole, or a lacy bra, or maybe just the outline of the woman herself. He was a sucker for fancy lingerie. Not the bawdy stuff like animal prints, or anything obvious like black leather cut-outs. But soft, expensive, sweet, barely there bras and panties undid him.

Declan's only intention had been to walk Joey to the door, meet the wife that Joey never stopped talking about when the two men talked on the phone, say goodbye, and return to the party. The party was in his honor, and it would be rude to spend too much time with any one guest, but this woman made Declan quickly change his mind. With an eerie sense of knowledge, he knew that she could pull him from his self-imposed funk.

He had to get to know her better, and if the look of distaste on her face as she watched one of his teammates openly grope some girl meant anything, he didn't think he could talk her out of skipping the restaurant and staying at the party with him.

As if calling an audible at the line, Declan had hurriedly changed the play. "I'm coming to dinner with you guys, if that's okay," Declan quietly said to Joey as they had neared the women.

"Sure. Of course. That'd be great, but…yeah…okay, whatever. Great," Joey said, obviously surprised at Declan's announcement.

Now, still holding her hand, Declan thought that maybe that was the best play he'd called all day. Yes, it was definitely a thunderbolt that went through Declan. He slowly released Marlee's hand and gave her his best killer smile. Her hand had been cold, probably from just coming in, and it had warmed in the small amount of time that Declan had held it. He regretfully let it slip from his, making a silent promise to himself to not let this woman get cold again tonight.

"It's *Ms.* Reeves. But please call me Marlee."

Damn, the Ms. thing. That could mean anything. He surreptitiously glanced at her left hand. No ring of any kind; that was good. She could have a boyfriend, though. He grimaced to himself. Well, they'd have a nice, long, drawn-out dinner if he had anything to say about it, and he'd get to know her better.

She seemed so different from all the women he knew. He was intrigued with her. He knew it was a cliché, but he was dying to slide off her glasses, take the pins out of her hair, have her shake it out, and become a wildcat right in front of him. She had the green-gold eyes of a cat—and the grace of one, as well. He had noticed that right away—the way she moved, her ease. She had walked into a room full of people that she didn't know, that she was 180 degrees different from, and seemed not to notice or care.

"I'm going to go back, leave through the kitchen and out the back. I'll meet you in the driveway. What kind of car are you driving?" Declan asked Kathy and Marlee, not sure which one of the women had driven to the party.

"Kathy has my rental car," Joey said. "It's a white Escalade." As Declan nodded, they started to turn, Joey and Kathy toward the front door, and Declan back toward the party.

"Wait, I'm confused. Why do you have to go through the kitchen?" Marlee asked, puzzlement on her pretty face.

"I don't want anyone to know I'm leaving the party," Declan explained.

"Why?" Marlee still wasn't grasping what the other three seemed to find a perfect plan.

"Because it's my party. My house," Declan said as he

turned and started his journey. He looked back to see Marlee still looking confused. He returned to her, took her hand, and held it in his own for a moment. The thunderbolt was back. It hadn't been a fluke the first time.

He looked into her eyes and knew she felt it too. How could she not when it almost knocked him off his feet?

He leaned close, his breath kicking up wisps of Marlee's hair as he spoke. He tried to gently explain to Marlee who he was, not wanting to scare her off. He wasn't sure how he knew that his identity would not be welcome knowledge to her, but it was something he sensed.

"I'm Declan Tate, Marlee." Marlee nodded. Yes, she had caught his name during Joey's introductions, so what? "This is my house. I'm the quarterback of the Boston Pumas. This is my team. Today was my last game ever, and if they realize I'm leaving my own farewell party so that I can get to know a beautiful woman I've just met, they are not going to be happy. And believe me, you do not want to make these guys unhappy." Declan turned and once more tried to make his exit.

Chapter 2

Marlee stared after Declan, dumbfounded. She vaguely remembered the name Tate on the public address system at the game today, but she had been so overwhelmed just trying to figure out the basics of the game that she quickly gave up on names and just looked at the players' jersey numbers. Even that had been a futile attempt to absorb the game. After a while, Marlee had just given up and caught up with Kathy. Joey had watched the game from the sidelines, and although they could have sat in Joey's friend's private box, not knowing anyone else that would be there, she and Kathy had chosen to sit in regular seats with the rest of the crowd.

The stands had been full mostly of men, but there was a good number of families too, and that was what Marlee's eye kept returning to as she and Kathy chatted. One family especially drew her in. The mother looked to be a few years older than her, the father about the same age. They had a son who looked to be around five. The father held his son on his lap most of the game while he tried to explain to him the finer points. It was obvious that even at five, the boy had a much better handle on football than Marlee did.

Was this what she would do when she had a family, Marlee had daydreamed? Would they go to outings every weekend? Certainly not football, but some other event. They'd bundle up the kids to brave the Boston winters, get them cocoa and a hot dog. She'd always remember to bring Wet Ones, like this mother had, for the perpetual ketchup and chocolate rings around the mouth. The boy had kept yelling something. What had it been? Oh yes: "Atta boy, Declan."

Oh God. Marlee realized that boy had meant her Declan.

Shuddering at the ease at which she thought of him as *her* Declan, Marlee's eyes were once again drawn to the man as he made his way across the room.

His room. Full of his people.

From her perch in the raised foyer, Declan looked like a salmon trying to swim upstream, the huge linemen from his team waves that he crashed against. People stopped him with handshakes and hugs, some of the huge men actually crying— much to Marlee's astonishment—as they spoke with their leader.

Women threw their arms around him, hugging and kissing him. Marlee noticed more than one woman slip a piece of paper in Declan's hand, which he would then slip into his pants pocket. One even went so far as putting a slip of paper in the front pocket of his pants herself, sliding her hand across his crotch and giving him a little pat.

An unease settled upon Marlee. She was out of her league here, amongst the aggressive—both in dress and action— women. She could not compete with such women. She *would* not compete with them. She was almost sick to her stomach thinking about how similar this scene was to one that had played out two years ago. She wanted to turn and run, but she could not take her eyes off of Declan.

He finally made it to the arched entranceway at the back of the room, which Marlee assumed led to the kitchen. She wouldn't get to see it after all, but that was okay. Her need to leave this house overrode her curiosity. She wanted to get away from these people—the loud, physically overbearing men and the sexually aggressive women. It was like high school with money.

He turned, saw her watching him, and smiled and waved to them, assuring that he had made a clean break. He motioned to them—twirling his long fingers in a circle—to leave and that he'd meet them outside.

Joey, Kathy, and Marlee turned and headed to the front door. They hadn't been inside very long and the coat check girl still had their coats out. She wore a cute little uniform, sort of French maid, and once again Marlee was jarred at the stab of…*jealousy?*…that the thought of this girl, and those women inside, did to her now that she'd met Declan. Now that she knew that this lovely house was his home, and that all these women were here at his invitation.

Coat check girl, valet parking when they had come in… Marlee had also seen several wait people circulating around the living room with trays of food and drink. The man spared no expense. Of course not. Though the home was much more modest than she would have thought, he was still an NFL star, and thus would be dripping with money, and eager to show it off.

Joey helped both women on with their coats. Kathy a sensible parka and Marlee's long camel hair coat that she wore to the university most days over her suits. Kathy had told her to dress warmly, but this was the heaviest coat she owned. She had never been outside for four hours in one sitting in a

Boston January. She was a Boston native, though she'd spent several years in California, first at Berkeley and then San Diego. But she'd been back in Boston long enough that she should have known better.

"How can you not know who Declan Tate is?" Kathy asked Marlee. Joey held the same incredulous expression as Kathy handed the valet her parking stub. "We watched him all day. It was Tate Day at the stadium because of it possibly being his last game; how could you not have noticed it? They were giving away Tate bobble heads, for goodness' sake."

"So…he's a football player?" was Marlee's weak reply.

"Not 'a' football player, 'the' football player. Sixteen-year pro career, the last five with the Pumas. Two Super Bowl rings, one in which he was the MVP, ten Pro Bowls, four-time league MVP…he's Declan Tate!" Joey was listing off Declan's stats, but Marlee had ceased to listen.

He was a professional athlete. Dear God, not again.

The attraction Marlee had felt slid from her like a snake sheds a layer of skin, and she felt just as slimy. A sports star, sure to have a groupie in every city, and a different one every night. She wondered how many nerdy boys he had pushed into lockers during his lifetime.

As she wrapped her arms around herself to try to stay warm, her mind wandered back to her stint as tutor to a football player when she was in high school. The first time in her life she'd had any kind of contact with an elite athlete.

Marlee had tutored Troy Stepovich the fall of their junior year in an attempt to keep Troy eligible for football. When their sessions first began, he flirted outrageously with the then-shy Marlee, taking great delight in making her blush. Toward the end of their sessions, he had toned down his style, if not his intentions. He was sweet and sensitive with her, holding her hand under the table as they studied in the privacy of the coach's office. She knew Troy could barely read beyond a seventh-grade level, but that didn't matter to Marlee. Not when Troy would rub her back as she tried to explain the different triangles to him. They never saw each other outside of their sessions—Troy had said he needed to concentrate on football, that with Marlee's help he could get a scholarship to play Division One football. She didn't care; she only wanted those sessions with Troy to never end.

But end they did, right after the football season. Elated with the idea that now that football was over they could spend more time together, Marlee waited for Troy at his locker the first Monday morning after the last game. He came toward her and she saw he was holding hands with Nicole Baranski, the head cheerleader. Marlee wasn't in the loop with the social crowd, didn't know how long they had been a couple—if indeed they were a couple—and then she noticed Troy's class ring on Nicole's hand. Well-worn red yarn wrapped around the band making it fit on her petite fingers.

Marlee stood in front of his locker, searching his handsome face, waiting for an explanation. None came. He only said, "Excuse me, that's my locker," and waited for Marlee to move. She did, going numbly through the rest of the day, and crying to her older sisters that night in the privacy of her bedroom.

The rest of the year and her entire senior year, Marlee did everything to avoid Troy, which wasn't too hard, as they shared none of the same classes or extracurricular activities. When she did have the misfortune to see him in the halls, he'd inevitably have his huge arms draped around Nicole. Either he didn't even notice Marlee as he made his way past her, or he pretended not to know her. She wasn't sure which idea hurt more.

And as if she hadn't learned her lesson, she'd had an even

more catastrophic experience with a professional athlete two years ago. She still couldn't think about that without her heart —and pride—taking a beating.

The blast of cold air as they left Declan Tate's house brought Marlee back from her thoughts of the past, and back to Declan.

She couldn't believe that she was so attracted to a football player. She felt as if she had been duped, misled by Declan's comparatively smaller stature, his attire, and what Marlee interpreted as a keen intellect. Right. Exactly what part of him screamed intellect? His gorgeous chestnut hair? The perfect white teeth in his perfect white smile? The eyes so green they looked like…*Enough!*

All thoughts—however brief—of Declan and her emulating the family she'd seen at the game went up in smoke. There would be no hot chocolate and Wet Ones for Declan and her. She simply would not settle in her quest for a man with whom to share her vision of family. Outwardly, Declan appeared ready for the starring role. But he was a football player. He had to have women everywhere, some willing to do anything to be with him. She could never be comfortable with that kind of man.

She would not go through that again.

She reluctantly slid Declan Tate from the "Lots of Possibilities" to the "Don't Go Near Him With a Ten-Foot Pole" column in her mind.

Still, Marlee couldn't shake the feeling of regret as the valet pulled up the car and they got in. Kathy sat in the front with Joey, while Marlee entered the back. Her regret rapidly turned into resentment. She knew it wasn't logical, but she became mad at Declan Tate for being a famous football player, and obviously a major *playah* if the array of women in his home was any indication. She'd had a momentary flash of—a future?…a relationship?—*something* with this man, all to have it dashed away with the knowledge that he was a huge sports star surrounded by women.

Yeah, she knew it was crazy, but that was how she felt. The cold must have seeped into her brain at the game.

They only had to wait a moment until Declan came from behind the house and joined Marlee in the back seat. He gave her a smile, put his hand over hers that had been resting on the seat between them, gave it a quick squeeze, and released it.

Marlee's breath caught, but she quickly regained her composure. She pulled her hand to her lap and turned her head away, looking out the car window as they headed off to the restaurant. Her hand tingled. She was deluding herself if she thought it was from the cold and not Declan's touch.

She needed to convey the message to him that their mutual attraction had ended as quickly as it had begun. At least on her part. Marlee decided that if she told herself that as many times as possible before they reached the restaurant, she might actually start to believe it.

WHAT THE HELL HAPPENED, DECLAN WONDERED? HE'D had enough experience with women in his life to know when there was chemistry. There had definitely been chemistry with Marlee, and it hadn't been all on his side, either. He knew she'd felt the same thing he had when they'd shook hands. He had been reluctant to let hers go. It fit so nicely in his, a complement to his own. He could easily envision holding her hand, how they would fit together. Also, he could have sworn she'd made some kind of little sound just now as he squeezed her hand. A pleasurable sound.

He was about to put his arm around her when she took her hand away and turned her head to stare out the window. It was pitch black out, for Christ's sake—what was she looking at? Or did she just not want to look at him? Shy? Declan didn't think so; he hadn't read that about her from the way she carried herself. She seemed very confident, in control of herself. She had met him head on, reaching for his hand to shake first, before he could react to her. No, not shy. What, then? Why the about-face from when he left her in the living room until he got into the car with her?

Declan mentally retraced his steps. All had been fine until they had separated at the party, she to go out the front, he to go out the back. Could she have met someone in the short time it took him to get to the car? Unlikely. But what could have happened? She had been surprised to learn he was Declan Tate. No, that wasn't it. She had been surprised to learn who Declan Tate *was*—a football player. Could that be it?

Declan tried a different tack, determined to re-stoke the fire that she'd so abruptly extinguished. "So, Marlee, what do you do for a living?"

Marlee didn't turn her head toward Declan, but she at least turned away from the window to stare straight ahead. "I'm a professor at Boston College."

"Marlee, don't be so modest," Kathy piped in from the front seat. She turned around to face Declan as she expanded on Marlee's brief description. "She's one of the most respected professors at Boston College. She teaches communication theory. Particularly speech. In addition to that, Marlee has worked with some of the top politicians on speech behavior. Taught a bunch of famous people how to give effective speeches. People in the tech field who might not be so good at public speaking. That sort of thing. I guess you could say she's the Declan Tate of speech gurus."

"Except I don't have groupies," Marlee added, a little too sharply for Declan's taste.

"Aahh. So that's why the deep freeze? Because of the groupies?"

"I don't know what you're talking about," Marlee answered. She put as much conviction behind it as she could, but it still sounded lame to Declan.

Joey and Kathy exchanged glances and Kathy turned to face the front once more. Joey shot him a look in the rearview, and Declan gave a slight shake of his head. They didn't know what was happening in the back seat, but they knew they were better off staying out of it. And Declan was grateful for that.

Shit, Declan didn't know himself what was going on in the back seat. But part of him was enjoying it.

He'd tried the diversion tactic, asking about her work, and he was impressed, but he needed to get back to the game at hand. If she was still playing dumb, he'd bring on the full blitz.

"You know exactly what I'm talking about with the deep freeze. We had, I don't know…a moment…back at my house. Something happened and I know you felt it too. Then I get in the car and you're the Ice Queen. Is it because you realized I play football or because you realized all those women are groupies and they're at *my* house?"

He did slide his arm around her shoulders then, but not in the soft, cuddling way he had intended earlier. This time he used his arm to propel her into facing him, curling his powerful forearm to hold her tight. He wasn't one for strong-armed tactics, and certainly not with women, but this situation called for it.

"You can have whomever you choose at your house. It's no concern of mine. I don't even know you."

"That's right, I can. And you don't know me. But had I known I was going to meet you, and that we'd have this… connection, it would never have been under those circumstances. I'm not interested in those girls; they just come with the team, I didn't invite them. It's been a long time since I was a rookie, interested in that kind of stuff. I just wanted to have a little party to thank my linemen for all they've done for me. But the after-game parties are never little. I don't know why I was hoping this one would be." And it was true, what he'd said about not inviting the girls, and also what he'd said about it being a long time since he'd enjoyed that sort of thing.

Declan had been wild his first few seasons, taking advantage of the beautiful women—girls, really—who followed the NFL players. He had indulged in all the excesses the league had to offer, many of them with Joey Robinson as his sidekick. In his fourth season, after being benched for most of the year, his coach had told him he was being traded.

"If you could just be as focused as I know you could be, you'd be one of the greats, Declan, but you love the partying and the girls too much. I'm just not willing to bet that you'll grow out of it." Declan had been traded to the worst team in the league, and it had been the wake-up call he needed.

His focus became solely football. He spent his off-seasons at his parents' farm in Ohio, getting up at the crack of dawn, working out, throwing footballs through hung tires for hours on end, working side by side with his father in the fields, and going to bed at dusk. Alone.

He shunned the nightlife that went along with being an NFL star. He turned down all endorsements, thinking they'd take away from his focus of the game. He steered clear of the fast women, preferring to date quietly, never getting serious with any one woman.

They were always available, and they weren't all as trampy-looking as the women who were presently at his house. But the majority of women Declan met, he met through some facet of the game. The hangers-on, the cheerleaders—though that was a league no-no that never stopped Declan—the friends of teammates' wives, looking to become a player's wife themselves.

His desire for women hadn't waned, and he had more than his fair share, but it wasn't as decadent and debauched as it had been his first few seasons. No more twins. Or triplets.

Eight years later he was traded again, this time to Boston. And this time it was an incredible trade, because Declan had indeed become one of the all-time great quarterbacks of the game. It was $180 million/five-year deal that, at the time, had broken all records.

Now his five years were up, and though the franchise begged him to stay on, he wanted to go out while he could still run off the field, not limp. His body was thirty-nine years old—prime for most other professions, but over the hill for the NFL. The hits he took would wake him at night, keeping him from any real rest. Bruises would just begin to fade by the next game, only to be re-administered.

And he didn't even want to think about any damage concussions might have done.

He also didn't want to stick around just to be some Yoda-like guru to an up-and-comer that would take his place. He'd pass on his knowledge and wisdom, all right, but hopefully to a son, not some son-of-a-bitch who was waiting for Declan to break a leg.

They rode in silence and Marlee squirmed a bit against Declan, but he didn't want to take his arm from around her. He was afraid she'd slide back into the corner of the SUV and face the window again. And damn, he just liked keeping a hold on her. Most of the women he was with were petite things. Marlee had some size on her. Tall and sturdy, something substantial to hold. Or hold on to, as he was now doing.

They arrived at the restaurant and got out so the valet

could take the car, and Marlee, pushing her glasses up her nose, looked up to see they were at one of Boston's famed steakhouses. Kathy noticed at the same time.

"Joey, Marlee is a vegetarian," Kathy said quietly. "Maybe we could walk down the block and find someplace else?"

"No, that's okay. I'm sure I can get a salad here, it's no problem," Marlee said.

Declan figured Marlee assumed he would be downing the largest, rarest steak at the restaurant. Possibly with his bare hands.

"They have a great house salad here. That's how I know about this place. Declan is a vegetarian too," Joey explained.

Marlee swung her head at Declan, stunned.

Declan immediately deciphered Marlee's look. "What's the matter, being a vegetarian doesn't fit in the pigeonhole you've put me in?" Declan knew he was being overly snide, but he'd been stung by Marlee's obvious dismissal of him.

"You're right, I did assume you were a carnivore, but then so is ninety percent of the U.S. population." Marlee was gracious in her apology, if just a little smug. She had rambled the statistic out with so much authority that no one would question it.

He would question it. Question her.

"Actually, ninety-seven percent are carnivore. The remaining three percent are a combination of vegetarians and vegans. Shall we go in?"

He took her elbow and guided her through the door, not giving her a chance to respond to his rebuttal. He cast a sideways glance at her and was happy to see she seemed flustered. Declan couldn't be sure if that was from his unexpected vegetarian status, his knowledge on the subject, or from him simply touching her.

Damn, but touching her sure made *him* flustered. Even her frickin' elbow felt sexy.

He could feel the strong pull of arousal beginning in his abdomen. If he kept his hands on her, it would be just a matter of time before he was sporting a full-fledged hard-on. Declan couldn't remember, but he silently prayed that the restaurant had long tablecloths. He needed a shield, because he had no intention of keeping his hands off Marlee.

He was perceptive to the fact that touching her aroused not only him, but Marlee as well. It was as if he could keep her from thinking too much by using direct contact. It might keep her off-kilter long enough for him to combat this icy-cool façade she'd put in place. He, more than anyone, knew that the best defense was a good offense.

"Dude, what's the deal?" Joey asked as he pulled Declan aside while they passed through the coat check area. "What was going on back there?"

Declan looked at his good friend. He'd played with a lot of guys over the years, and had partied with a bunch of them. None more so than Joey Robinson back in the day. He was glad he and Joey had always stayed in touch even after they both went to different teams.

He shook his head as he answered. "I don't really know. I just know that I—we—felt something at my house. And then she totally shut me down in the car."

Joey stood toe to toe with him. Joey was a linebacker and had a good four inches and fifty pounds of muscle on Declan. "If she shuts you down, you stay down. She's a friend of Kathy's and you can't pull any of your shit with her."

Declan looked at his friend. He hadn't spent any time with Joey since he'd met and married Kathy. "Dude, marriage has changed you."

Joey shook his head. "Not marriage, man. Love. Love changed me."

It had. Declan could see that now. "That's great, man. Really great."

Joey smiled, but still stayed in Declan's face. "Yeah, it is. And if Kathy's friend gets pissed, then my sweet Kathy gets pissed. And if that happens, then I get pissed. And I *know* you've seen me get pissed…and it ain't pretty."

"Amen to that," Declan said. He put a hand on his friend's bulging bicep. "It won't get that far, I promise. If she's really not into me, I'll back off. But"—he ran his hand through his hair, then looked at Joey—"I've got to try. It was too damn good when I held her hand to not imagine how good it could be if it became anything more."

Joey studied him for a second, then slowly nodded. "Good enough." He stepped out of Declan's way, waving him forward. "This should be interesting."

The restaurant was dark, with the only discernible lighting coming from the large candles on each table. The tables were of various sizes, but all round. White linen tablecloths were accented with blood-red napkins. It was a warm, jovial atmosphere. It was a family-oriented steakhouse, typically filled with older couples and young families. Declan had discovered it his first year in Boston and came at least once a week, making friends with Gino, the owner.

Many of the diners seemed to recognize Declan as they stood at the hostess stand, handing their coats to Joey to hang up. There was much murmuring, and then, as if on cue, the entire place erupted into a round of applause. Most of the men stood up. Declan took the outcry of emotion in stride. He hung his head, and then raised it with a wide smile. He gave a little wave of appreciation to them all. After all these years he was still humbled and honored by the devotion he felt from people.

"*Paisan!*" Gino greeted Declan. "I'm so honored you'd come here tonight of all nights! It was a shame your final game was a loss, but what can you do when the other team scores fifty-four points?"

"Score fifty-five?" Declan said with a smile on his face.

It was true that the Pumas' defense was horrible this season, but Declan had always been a fierce competitor. He had learned to outwardly take defeat graciously, but inside his stomach would churn for days after a loss. He'd watch hours upon hours of tape, trying to see if there was one thing he could have done differently to change the outcome of the game. Then he'd start watching more tape of the upcoming team.

No more. There was now an end to all the time spent in dark screening rooms with a remote in his left hand and his right hand furiously scribbling notes. Sometimes it was a tossup as to which had more of an adverse effect on his throwing hand: hurtling a hundred passes during practice, or writer's cramp from his nightly dissections.

"Let me get you our best table." Gino was shaking hands with Declan, but before he could turn away on his quest for the perfect table, Declan pulled him close to whisper something in his ear.

Gino quickly looked at Marlee, then glanced at Declan, smiled, and nodded. "Right this way. I know just the spot."

Marlee gave Declan a look that indicated she wondered what he was up to. Declan just smiled in response. As Marlee passed Declan to follow Gino, he quickly stepped in stride with her and clasped her hand. She didn't even seem surprised, and only slightly tried to pull away. Progress, Declan thought, as he held on tight.

Gino led them to the back of the restaurant to a dimly lit, round-tabled booth with high backs. There were few diners at the surrounding tables, the corner being very private. Gino gracefully pulled the table out to allow Kathy and Marlee to slide around to the back. Marlee had to disengage her hand from Declan, and he felt an ache as she did.

After sliding the table back in, Gino turned to Declan before he could slide in next to Marlee. "*Paisan*, could I impose on you to come back and say hello to Serge?" he asked with a smile.

"Serge is cooking tonight? Absolutely. No imposition whatsoever." He turned to the women, but his eyes were on Marlee. "Ladies, will you excuse me for a minute?" They both nodded, and Declan was happy to see a look that resembled regret in Marlee's eyes. "It'll only take a second, but Serge and I go way back. Plus, if I say hello, I can guarantee you the most heavenly dinner you've ever had."

Both Kathy and Marlee smiled, Kathy making a dismissive shooing motion with her hands. "By all means, then. Tell him to go heavy on the cheese on my order," Kathy said. Marlee only smiled and nodded, but it was a heck of a lot more than he got in the car.

Yep, definite progress.

"Well then, I might as well make a trip to the boys' room," Joey said.

Declan and Joey trailed after Gino, leaving the women alone.

THE WOMEN'S EYES FOLLOWED THE MEN. THE SECOND they were out of earshot, Kathy turned to Marlee. "What the heck is going on?"

Marlee didn't pretend not to know what Kathy was

talking about. She slouched back against the padded booth, letting her head rest on the back of the seat. "I don't know? I…I…I don't know." She closed her eyes, but her mind was filled with images of Declan, so she quickly opened them again.

"He's all over you. *Declan Tate* is all over you," Kathy exclaimed. "I mean, I could see it even at his house, the way the two of you couldn't take your eyes off each other, as if you were eating each other up."

Marlee had a flash of her mouth fused to Declan's, and she let out a groan. "I know. It was so weird, Kathy, I can't explain it. And when he shook my hand…" Marlee raised the hand in question to look at it, as if to show Kathy the brand that Declan had left on her.

Across the restaurant, she saw Declan coming out of the kitchen. He started on his way back but was waylaid by nearly every table. The men jumping out of their seats to shake his hand. Declan was polite, stopping and chatting with each group. He met Marlee's eyes and shrugged in an apologetic way.

A memory from two years ago played in her mind, and the truth of her current situation came crashing down on Marlee. "But then I realized he's a football player," she said, almost to herself.

"Well, of course he's a football player. So what?" Kathy asked incredulously. "So is Joey."

Marlee shrugged. "There's no future in it. At least not for me."

Kathy was quiet, then softly said, "I know you were really burned by a jock before, Marlee. And I know you're looking for a future at this point in your life. But…"

Marlee looked away from watching Declan and to Kathy. "But what?"

"But maybe you can postpone your future for a night," Kathy gently said.

"You mean a one-night stand?"

"One night. Two nights. A couple of weeks."

"It wouldn't be a couple of weeks, anyway. I leave next week for my meetings in DC, remember?"

Kathy's face lit up. "All the better. You can have a one-week fling and then go to DC and wow them on the Hill. When you come back you can start looking for Mr. Right. But my God, Marlee, is there a better Mr. Right Now than Declan Tate?"

Marlee chuckled at her friend's insistence. "Kathy, I don't do flings."

Kathy's smile dropped. "Maybe it's time you did."

"What do you know about him, Kathy? Besides his football stats."

Kathy thought for a moment. "You know, not much, really. His reputation is one for all business when it comes to football. He doesn't do any endorsements. You never read about him dating an actress or a supermodel. In fact, you don't read much about his personal life period. He keeps a pretty low profile. The Tate temper is famous, but only on the field.

"Joey played with him a while ago, and they keep in touch, but I don't know that Declan has lots of friends. I get the impression from Joey that during the season Declan keeps pretty much to himself."

Remembering all those women in Declan's home made Marlee question that last bit of information. Remembering how those women looked and how young they were made Marlee question her sanity at even considering Kathy's suggestion of a fling.

As Declan finally made his way past the throng of admirers, Kathy said softly, "Think about it, Marlee—when would you ever have this chance again? And let me just add… sex with a pro athlete? All that stamina and muscle? Unbelievable."

Marlee knew that firsthand. She just wasn't sure she was strong enough to again go through all the bullshit that went with it.

Chapter 3

Marlee's and Kathy's voices abruptly dropped off as Declan was finally able to get to the table. It was obvious they'd been talking about him. His gut clenched for a moment as he wondered what the verdict was. He turned to Marlee with a raised, questioning brow. "And what did you ladies find to talk about?"

Joey got back to the table at the same time, and the men both sat down. He'd run his own semi-gauntlet of fans, but wasn't as recognizable in Boston as Declan was. Declan scooted close to Marlee; Joey did the same on the other side of the table to be near Kathy. He draped his large arm over his petite wife, who snuggled into his side, giving Declan a small pang of envy.

"Oh, nothing much," Marlee said, but then a small smile lit her face and she bowed her head to keep Declan from noticing.

But he noticed. She didn't *want* to like him. She had something against him, but damn if she didn't like when he touched her. To prove his point, he once again took her hand, and placed both his and her entwined hands on his thigh. He moved them gently back and forth, not sure if he was doing so to excite Marlee or himself. Did it matter? His thigh, solid muscle from years of workouts, nearly liquefied as her hand, albeit with his guidance, lightly stroked.

Thankfully, the fine linen tablecloths went all the way to the floor. Declan said a silent hallelujah and began caressing Marlee's hand, beginning with the sensitive skin between her thumb and forefinger. Her fingers were long and elegant. So were his, he knew, all the better to wrap around a football. What would Marlee's digits be best wrapped around? Declan nearly choked on his ice water at the thought.

Marlee was quiet for a moment. It looked like she was silently contemplating something, her brows furrowed as if solving a problem. That must have been it, because she suddenly straightened her shoulders and lifted her chin. Decision made. But what had she been deciding?

She stroked her free hand up Declan's arm, turning her body into his, while she squeezed his hand that joined hers. Her cat-green eyes looked into his, so deep, so crystal clear he felt as though she could look through him. She locked them with his and simply said, "Yes."

Declan was mesmerized by her eyes, and it took him a moment to realize what she'd said. It took him a couple of seconds longer to deduce what Marlee was talking about. She was saying yes to him, wasn't she? Yes to *them*. Yes to being with him, getting under the sheets, getting under him, and getting down to business. Declan flashed her his trademark smile—the one he flashed when he'd just come back from ten points down with four minutes left to win the game—and leaned forward to kiss her.

He was interrupted by Joey, who, until this time, had his head stuck behind a menu, oblivious to Declan's and Marlee's deep gazes. "Yes what, Marlee? What was the question? I missed it."

Declan smiled at Marlee with regret that his proposed kiss had been cut short and turned to Joey, but had no intention of explaining. How could he explain something to Joey he didn't understand himself? Plus, after Joey's warning, he wasn't sure his buddy would be as happy about Marlee's answer as Declan was. "It was something I asked Marlee, Joey, and I got the answer I wanted."

"Yes. But on one condition," Marlee said, holding Declan's gaze.

Declan groaned playfully. "Of course there'd be a condition. I should have figured that with a woman like you. What's the condition?"

Marlee ignored Declan's "woman like you" comment. "Yes, if you can correctly guess how many slips of paper with phone numbers you have in your pants at this exact moment."

"Easy. None. Guess it's a qualified yes, then."

"I don't believe you. There must be at least five, probably more." He knew she'd seen the women hand him their numbers and Declan, in turn, had put them in his pants. He could tell she thought he was lying. The look of hurt on her face proved it.

"There's none, darlin', but you're more than welcome to find out for yourself." Declan freed his hand from hers and held his arms out from his body, to indicate he was ready for Marlee to frisk him. The loss of contact, and its adverse effect, shocked him. He wanted to reconnect immediately, but Marlee was insistent on the phone numbers.

"That won't be necessary." She turned away from him, back to Kathy and Joey, who were engrossed at the moment in their own conversation. Thank goodness. He didn't want her friends to hear what he was about to say to her.

Declan took Marlee's hand again and said quietly in her ear, "I trashed them all in the kitchen as I was leaving the house. I don't need anyone's number tonight, Marlee. I only want you."

MARLEE'S HEAD WAS SPINNING. DARN, SHE WAS RIGHT back where she was moments ago, wanting a man whom she had no business wanting.

He said he didn't want anyone else's number *tonight*. That was telling. Obviously he was thinking even shorter-term than she. That was fine; she'd just have to get her fill of Declan in one night. Hopefully it would just be a very long night.

Joey and Kathy's discussion ended at the same time Declan and Marlee had made their peace, and Joey turned to Marlee. "Hey, Marlee, what was it you wanted to talk to me about? Something to do with why you wanted to go to the game with us today, right?"

"Oh, well, I'll ask you some other time, Joey. It's really not that important."

Declan squeezed her hand. "What was it, sweetheart? What did you want to talk to Joey about?" As he said this, Declan disengaged their hands that had been previously hidden under the table, and put his arm around her shoulder. Out in the open now. Might as well let Joey and Kathy in on their secret.

They were going to be together. Probably only for tonight. But Declan seemed intent on letting everyone know it.

Joey and Kathy once again exchanged glances but didn't seem too surprised by Declan's PDA.

Marlee faced Declan, surprised that she kind of liked the "sweetheart." "It seems silly now, with you here, but the reason I wanted to go to the game today and the reason I want to pick Joey's brain is I want to learn more about the game of football."

"Well shoot, darlin'. You'll get two for the price of one tonight. Why do you want to know about football? And, better yet, why *don't* you know about football already? It's our national pastime, for Christ's sake."

"I thought that was baseball," Joey piped in.

"Whatever." Declan arrogantly waved Joey's statement away as he turned to face Marlee. He had begun absently stroking her shoulder and upper arm with his strong, callused thumb, and she found it soothing, hypnotic.

"Believe it or not, I've done more than okay in my thirty years without knowing a thing about football. It may be your entire life, but a lot of us out there couldn't care less about the sport."

"Okay. So why learn now, if you've done so fine before?"

"Kathy mentioned that I'm a communications professor?" At Declan's nod of acknowledgement, Marlee continued, "Next week I'm going to DC to speak with the education department about the need for more speech and public speaking, starting earlier in schools. From there I'm touring some universities to talk about it. How the onslaught of texting and social media has drastically decreased the ability for young people to do any kind of intelligent public speaking."

"True dat," Kathy said with a wink.

Marlee smiled at her and continued, "I don't do it a lot, but when I speak at other schools I usually do some kind of icebreaker, then I tie speech theories to it in a metaphorical way, and then I come back to it as I wrap up the lecture. In the past, my lectures have been attended by solely other faculty members of the universities where I'm speaking, so the interest points I weave through has been very, shall we say, cerebral, for lack of better term."

"Meaning I wouldn't have a clue what you were talking about?" Declan said, and they all laughed.

"This series of lectures will probably be different. Because of the Department of Education's interest on the topic, it's my understanding that there will be larger audiences of a more general makeup. And I'll want to have a more relatable icebreaker that I can then tie back around. So, the common denominator that I've come up with as a thread throughout my lecture is football."

"That's a great idea. Especially in college towns," Joey said.

"That's what I was thinking. If I can make it interesting enough, or state it in a way that appeals to the mass audience, I know I'll have a better response."

"So you want to cram up on football? Darlin', it's not that easy."

"I know, but I figured if I went to a game, then had Joey explain the basic theory behind it, I could come up with something. Tie the need for good public speaking skills to, I don't know, the need for a good…offense?"

Declan gave her a look like she'd just said something adorable. She figured she'd probably messed up even that small analogy.

He caught a wisp of her hair that had come down from her chignon. He twirled it around his finger. He motioned for the waiter. "Let's get our order in now, and then I'll tell you why your plan sucks."

Chapter 4

After a wonderful dinner comprised of a magnificent salad, full of feta, walnuts and dried cherries, and a loaf of fresh-from-the-oven bread, Declan turned to Marlee. He normally couldn't wait to have a glass of wine or two after his last game of the year. He abstained during the season, but he didn't order one tonight. He wanted his head clear with Marlee.

He'd taken his arm back so that he could eat, and now he placed his hand on her thigh. Very high up on her thigh. Her thigh was almost as firm as Declan's, and much more shapely. She must work out. Then why did she know nothing about sports? Probably tai chi or yoga or some such crap. Of course she'd have to wear pants tonight, Declan lamented. No skirt hem to gently ease up with his hand. Couldn't anything with this woman be easy? She was making his head spin more than seeing a nose guard bearing down on him.

"Marlee, true football people can smell a phony a mile off. If you, someone who knows absolutely nothing about the game, opens your lecture with a football anecdote, you'll lose all credibility right then and there. Then who's going to listen to you wax about the importance of—and breakdown of—public speaking, when all they're thinking to themselves is 'she meant tight end when she said right guard'?"

"How could I ever mix up a tight end and a right guard when I don't even know what either one is?"

"Exactly my point."

"So explain the difference to me."

"Marlee, I know to your educated eye football seems like a barbaric game where men just run willy-nilly around the field trying to hurt each other, but it's much more than that. The tactics, the precision, the strategy, the talent that is on that field is astounding."

She hesitated, then said, "I realize that."

"No, you don't. You don't realize that, you just don't want to piss me off because of what's happening between us. You don't want to sabotage it." She looked like she wanted to argue, but he quickly continued, "But let me be clear. We are going to happen, Marlee—I don't know for how long, but I do know it's going to be good. It's going to happen regardless of this football-as-it-applies-to-public-speaking discussion we're having, so you might as well speak your mind on the subject."

"Listen, we're going to take off, can you guys get home all right, or…" Joey said.

"We're good," Declan said to his friend. They shook hands, Declan standing and giving his former teammate a hug. "Thanks so much for coming today, man. With my family not here, it really meant a lot. I'm just sorry you had the Sunday off so you could make it."

"We'll make it further next year," Joey said, and Declan nodded. It was a fluke and an unlucky fumble that had the Lumberjacks out so early in the playoffs this year.

"You're…okay?" Kathy asked Marlee.

Declan watched the unspoken words that flashed across

the women's faces. It seemed Marlee had Kathy's approval, and even encouragement, to go home with him.

"I'm good," Marlee finally said. Kathy hugged her friend in the booth, then scooted out the other side, and the married couple left the restaurant.

Sliding back into the booth, even closer to her statuesque body than he'd been before, he asked, "Where were we?"

"Me learning football."

"Right. Or rather *not* being able to learn it over a dinner so that you could speak intelligently about it."

"I just think that I'd able to pick up the basics of the game, tailor it to my lecture, and that would be that. I don't need to know the philosophy of the game or its conception through current history just so I can have an icebreaker, for Pete's sake."

"You said you'll be lecturing at universities?"

"Yes."

"Major universities, small ones, junior colleges, what?" He played with her hair again, then let go of the tendril of hair and moved to her neck, softly stroking. She had a long, graceful neck that seemed to rise from her silky blouse like a tall aspen reaches for the sky. His fingers gently caressed, smoothing down the line of a translucent vein. Her skin was so soft, and he could just catch the scent of…jasmine.

"Mostly major universities, why?" She seemed flustered by his hand on her, her face flushing a cute shade of pink. But she moved her head slightly, giving him better access.

"Well, you know, the icebreaker you make at University of Florida might be a hit there, but a flop at Maryland. If you discuss texting as being as big an arch rival to public speaking as Michigan when you're at Miami, you'll flop. If you say the same thing at Ohio State, you'll have them enthralled. If you talk about speech in elementary schools as if it were a basic running game at UCLA, where they run nothing but the West Coast Offense, you'll get blank stares."

Declan got a blank stare of his own from Marlee.

"But Marlee, it could have a lot of potential. It's a great idea, really. Do you have a list of where you'll be speaking yet?"

"I have a complete itinerary at home, why?"

"I'll take a look at it. You tell me your thoughts on what you'd like to say, how you had planned to weave football terms into your lecture, and then I'll tailor it to each university for you. This could be fun. I loved college football. The rivalries were the greatest. The traditions. You don't get that in the pros. There's a purity to the game at that level you don't have anymore in the pros. Though, unfortunately, college football is a big business itself these days."

"I couldn't possibly ask you to do that for me, Declan. That would take up a lot of your time."

Yeah, time he could be spending in bed with her. Still, it could mean more that just one night with her. And he was beginning to think that one night with Marlee Reeves might not be enough.

"Actually, you hit me at the right time. I am now officially unemployed. I have to be in New York next Monday morning. I'm taking a flight out Sunday afternoon, but my time is yours until then. And I'd really like something to distract me this week, anyway."

"Distract you from what?"

"Monday I start working on an audition tape in New York. Then my agent shops it around to the networks. I'm spending all next week at meetings with FOX, CBS, ABC, NBC, and ESPN. I never did any endorsements throughout my career because I didn't want to distract myself at all, so I have absolutely no experience in front of the camera, other than press conferences after games, and those are always a blur to me. I have this horrible vision of getting in front of those cameras next week and freezing, nothing coming out. Or of just rambling."

That was his worst fear. Making an ass of himself. Declan had always been so confident of his abilities, knew exactly what he was capable of on the field. This unknown of his possible new direction in life was beginning to creep up on him.

He hadn't allowed himself to think much about it while there were still games to concentrate on. Now, just the thought of stepping in front of the cameras made him tense. Unwittingly, Declan squeezed Marlee's neck. It wasn't hard, but it took her by surprise and she let out a little squeak.

"Sorry, darlin'." He smoothed her skin where he had squeezed it. "See, I'm getting all tensed up just thinking about it. My agent says they'll have all sorts of experts there to help me through it, but…"

"Declan, my God, you'd be amazing on camera. I don't know what size the female audience for watching football broadcasts is, but it will triple when you're on the screen. Do you have any idea how gorgeous you are?" Realizing what she'd blurted out, Marlee ducked her head. Declan lifted her chin to look at him, and she saw what was surely a smug smile. "Apparently you *do* know how gorgeous you are." She nudged him in his gut, causing a small grunt.

"But it's certainly nice to know that *you* think I am."

"So if you think you'd be so bad at this, why are you doing it?" she asked him.

Declan shrugged. "It's what ex-quarterbacks do. We go on TV and tell America how it should have been done."

"And you can do that?"

"Tell them how it should have been done? Sure. That was always my strength: strategy, play breakdowns, tactics, play-calling, I can do that in my sleep. The thought of being on camera to do it…that makes me nervous."

"The great Declan Tate nervous, I don't believe it. You play in front of cameras every week."

He waved a hand in dismissal. "That's different. I don't even know they're there. And three hours ago you had no idea who 'the great Declan Tate' was, so don't pull that bullshit with me."

"Three hours. I've only known you for three hours, and now…" She let the thought go, but Declan picked up the fumble and ran with it.

"And now we're going to sleep together. We are moving pretty fast, aren't we? I'm not going to lie and tell you I've never slept with a woman on the night I met her. Because I have, several times. I will tell you that I've never been the aggressor in those situations, it was always very easy for me. You're not an easy woman, Marlee, and I don't just mean sexually. That's obvious.

"I'm not going to get all flowery, either, and start spouting words that you and I both know I don't mean. I will tell you this. I have never been as immediately attracted to a woman as I am to you, Marlee. And I think it goes both ways. I'm only in town until Sunday, and you leave soon after that. We could have a great time scratching this itch that's been irritating us since we laid eyes on each other. I know that's not your usual style. You probably take things much slower, and I appreciate that, but Marlee…do you really want to slow down?"

He was giving her an out, but damn he hoped she wouldn't take it.

"No, I don't want to slow down. In fact, how fast can we get out of here?"

Declan had her out the booth and had Gino calling for a cab before she could take another breath.

HE NUZZLED HER NECK AS THEY STOOD IN THE DARK vestibule of the restaurant while they waited for their cab. He balanced her coat in the crook of his elbow, wanting her in as few layers as possible until their cab arrived and they had to brave the cold. His hands ran up and down her back, lower to her thighs, and once again he cursed her choice of pants over skirt. He really wanted to get his hands on her skin, but she was completely covered. She certainly left more to the imagination than most of the women he knew. He found he liked that. Liked having to imagine the shape and size of Marlee's breasts, not having them shoved in his face in a barely concealing top.

He undid the buttons of her suit coat and slipped his hand in to feel her smooth silk blouse. He rested his hand on her tummy. "God, Marlee, I can't wait to get you home, I need to get these clothes off you."

Marlee seemed distracted, and not only by Declan's hands on her. "Declan, I think I could help you."

"I know you can help me, baby, but not here, and not in the cab, either. I want you bad, but I don't want the driver getting off on our exploits. Or selling photos to TMZ."

Marlee giggled. God, what a cute sound she made when she did that.

"Not with that. Though I'll help you with *that* later. I was thinking about your audition. Do you think practicing in front of a camera and getting some feedback from me would put you more at ease about next week? I am good at what I do, you know."

Declan brought his head up from where it seemed permanently attached to Marlee's neck and thought about what she had just said. "Yeah, I think that would help. Do you have access to something like that, or were you thinking of home movies? Because, baby, I could think of lots of ways to film you and me together." He raised his eyebrows in a suggestive but kidding manner that made Marlee smile. God, what a smile she had. And that mouth: full lips that came to a perfect bow on top. Oh, what that sexy mouth could do to him.

"As a matter of fact, I have carte blanche at a video recording studio at Boston College for the week. I was going to tape my lecture and do self-critiques. We could do you as well. My experience is more in front of live audiences, but I've done my share with recording. I could give you some pointers."

"Would that interfere with your preparations?" What was he saying? She was giving him a chance to be around her for the whole week. *Grab it, man, grab it.* "I mean, that would be great. We could put the football stuff in your lecture at the same time."

"Great. I have the studio from ten to five every day this week. We can start tomorrow."

"Well, we won't be there by ten tomorrow."

"Why not?'

"Because I don't intend to let you out of bed until noon," he said as a cab pulled up to take them home.

Chapter 5

At quarter to ten the next morning, Marlee entered the Comm/Arts building and let herself into the video studio. Marlee's Chestnut Hill home was only a few minutes' drive from the Boston College campus, but this morning she had decided to walk to the studio. She did this frequently in the early fall and late spring, when she would spend the journey contemplating her classes and students, upcoming lectures, and even spend a few minutes thinking about her life.

It was on one such walk last fall, amidst the swirling, crisp, fallen orange leaves, that Marlee had come to the conclusion that she was ready to settle down and start a family. She would never give up teaching; she loved that too much. But once she had children, she would cut back to teaching only one or two classes a semester.

She'd thought she was ready two years earlier, but the dream had been ripped away from her, and it'd been too painful for her to think about again until recently.

It was shortly after that walk last fall that Marlee began driving through different suburbs and subdivisions, getting ideas of where she and her new family would ultimately live. She loved the home she currently owned, but she would want something larger once she had children.

She also began accepting more invitations to faculty social gatherings. Marlee assumed that her potential future mate would be met at just such a function, visualizing him as someone very much like herself: an academic who had reached professional achievement and was now ready to concentrate on home and hearth. So far the search had been fruitless, but Marlee had not been discouraged. It had only been a few months since she had come to her conclusion that she was ready to take a chance on love again.

Only this time with an appropriate man.

Marlee couldn't remember the last time she had walked to campus in the dead of winter. It had taken her a few minutes to uncover her heavy mittens and more substantial boots. And she felt the need for physical activity, because Lord knew she didn't get any last night.

Just as they were entering the cab, Declan's cell phone had rung.

"Sorry, I need to get that—only a few people have this number, and they wouldn't call if it wasn't important. Yeah, hello?"

Marlee watched from the back seat of the cab as Declan took in who was calling him, and his reaction as he seemed to grasp the reason for the call.

"If it's not that bad, can't you take care of it?" He stepped back on to the sidewalk, turned his back on Marlee, and said something softly into the phone that Marlee couldn't quite make out. After a few more moments of speaking softly into the phone, Declan's shoulders sagged. He turned around, and as he slipped his phone back into his jacket pocket, he informed Marlee, "I have to go home. You take this cab. I'll call another."

Without further explanation, Declan closed the backseat door on Marlee. He then opened the passenger-side door of the front and handed the cab driver a wad of bills. "Here you go; take her home, and please see that she gets inside safely. Could you please radio to your dispatch and have them send another cab here ASAP? I'll be going to Brookline." Declan looked to the back seat at a stunned Marlee. Just as she was about to protest his paying for her cab, he cut her off.

"I'm sorry, Marlee. You have no idea how sorry. I'll see you tomorrow morning, okay? At the studio? I know the Boston College campus pretty well; an old teammate of mine is the coach there. Which building will you be in?"

When Marlee described where the Comm/Arts building was located, and gave him the room number of the studio, Declan nodded in acknowledgement. "Yeah, I know where that is. Tomorrow at ten. I'll see you then. And Marlee, again, you have no idea how truly sorry I am that our night ended here." He closed the door and stepped to the curb, keeping his eyes on Marlee the entire time.

She only sat and stared at Declan, not knowing if she were relieved or disappointed at the turn of events. Her body was most definitely disappointed, but she suspected that it may have been too close a call for her heart.

Now, as Marlee began checking and setting up the video equipment, her body's endorphins kicking in from her walk, she surmised that it was probably divine intervention that had ended their evening as it had. She had almost slept with a man she had just met. A football player, no less! Someone with whom she had absolutely nothing in common.

A man *so* not appropriate for her future.

Marlee chided herself. She was a responsible adult—if she wanted to have a short fling with someone, as long as they were safe, and both willing, what was wrong with that? Why did she need more rationalization than being incredibly attracted to Declan, and he to her? She knew there was no future with a man like Declan, but she was entitled to a little fun, with a man who seemed to share in the mutual attraction.

At least, he was attracted to her last night. Maybe his lust was on time release and only lasted as long as his prey was within visual contact? Or maybe whoever had called him had assuaged that lust?

That was the crux of the matter. Who was it who called last night, and why did he feel the need to run to her? Her? It could just as easily have been a him. Marlee quickly replayed what she'd heard of Declan's conversation. No, he hadn't used any gender-specific terms. Marlee hadn't heard all of Declan's side, though, as he had turned away from her and his voice had gotten low and soft. Because he didn't want Marlee to hear, or because his listener was someone with whom Declan always used soft, low tones?

She couldn't stand the thought of Declan lumping her in with the many groupies he must encounter. He knew that she wasn't impressed by his athletic status; in fact, he must have realized that his prowess was a turn-off to Marlee. Yet she was still willing to go to bed with him hours after meeting him, and for only the possibility of one night. Where would that place her in Declan's lexicon of women? At groupie level? Slightly above? Surely not below. And if she only wanted one or two nights with him, why should it matter to Marlee what Declan thought of her?

But it did matter to her.

She was a respected professional, a conservative woman by

nature. She was no prude or virgin, but she'd never entered into what would certainly be a few-nights stand. There may have been a time, when she was younger, where she would have been more receptive to the "when I'm in town" relationship with an academic from another university, but to enter into that kind of arrangement now would only sidetrack her ultimate goal of marriage and children.

A knock on the locked door roused Marlee from her thoughts. She looked at her watch. Ten on the dot. She opened the door, and the sight of Declan once again took her breath away. Surely God must be a woman to create a man as gorgeous as Declan Tate. Or maybe the devil was involved, because the way he looked in well-worn blue jeans, a maroon henley, and a leather bomber jacket was downright sinful. A bright yellow knitted scarf that looked suspiciously homemade adorned his neck and hung forward onto his muscled chest. The scarf should look out of place on his *GQ* body, but it added a personal touch.

"Hi," was all the usually articulate Marlee could get out.

"Hi yourself."

He stepped into the studio, shut the door, made sure it was locked, and took Marlee in his arms. His cheek was cold against the top of her head. He smelled of snow and winter and leather jacket and something else Marlee couldn't name. Declan. He smelled of Declan.

He pulled back and held on to her upper arms, looking into her dazed eyes. She was still trying to decipher the glorious smell of him, and running through possible names of what she'd call it if she could bottle it. Stud? Quarterback? Winter Man? Nothing sounded quite right.

"Do you know what thought went through my head all last night?" he asked. As Marlee shook her head, Declan lightly touched her cheek. "I thought...my God, I never even got to kiss her. Over and over, like a mantra: 'I didn't get to kiss her, I didn't get to kiss her.' So, before some other emergency calls either one of us away, I'm going to make sure to put that one to rest."

Marlee's mind was still whirling from just the succulent sight of Declan, and it took her a moment to catch up with what he was saying. Before she could, Declan lowered his mouth to hers.

She'd been up most of the night as well, and like Declan, she'd thought of what hadn't happened. Unlike Declan, she had allowed her regret to surpass that of just a kiss. She had imagined them doing all sorts of steamy and wicked things, so that when Declan's soft mouth touched hers, she realized that she hadn't spent much time at all thinking about what kissing Declan would be like.

If she had thought his kiss would be strong, masculine, and aggressive—like Declan himself—she couldn't have been more wrong. Oh, it was strong, all right. But the strength was in its softness, its quiet determination. His lips at first just brushed hers. They were soft and warm, despite his having come in from a bitter Boston January morning. His scent once again filled her.

He angled his head a little to his right and went in for another brush. This time his delectable lips lingered on her mouth. He slowly opened his mouth and darted his tongue across her parted hers. Another soft, barely there caress and then he settled in to feast on her mouth.

She needed no guidance from him, and met his burning kiss head on. Their tongues tangled, gently at first, and then with a probing intensity. Marlee took Declan's tongue into her mouth and gently sucked on it. The taste of him was better than his scent. His tongue was rough, both salty and sweet.

Declan let out a harsh groan and tightened his hold on

Marlee as she wrapped her arms around his neck and pressed herself into him. Her hands came into contact with the yellow scarf, and the thought that she had never felt anything so soft in her life fleetingly went through her fogged brain. Declan shifted his weight, nudging her thighs apart and pressing himself into her. She'd never felt anything so hard in her life, as well.

Just as the need to rub herself against Declan's increasing erection was too much to bear, Declan pulled away from Marlee and gasped for breath. She was breathing hard as well and took a step back to compose herself.

She'd felt passion before, but had never gotten this worked up during a kiss, and a first kiss at that. She could feel the moistness in her panties, and her breasts felt heavy and unsatisfied. What this man did to her senses was alarming. But, Marlee argued with herself, if she was going to engage in a week-long fling with this him, didn't she want it to be mind-numbing? What was the sense of entering into an affair with someone who was totally wrong for her for just *meh* sex?

"God, Marlee, we've got to stop or we'll never get any work done. Come on." Declan took her hand and led her deeper into the studio, checking it out as he went. "The sooner we get done with our work, the sooner we can play."

He wiggled his brows suggestively at her and squeezed her hand. Marlee laughed in return. She hadn't expected a sly sense of humor from Declan, but he'd made her laugh several times throughout dinner last night. Marlee was slowly realizing that Declan Tate most certainly did not fit the mold that she had, admittedly unfairly, put him in.

DECLAN LOOKED AROUND THE ROOM. IT WAS A STUDIO about the size of a large living room. In the front of the room were three small sets placed side by side. Each set was on a carpeted platform that was a foot or so off the ground.

The first area was just a podium with a heavy maroon curtain hanging behind it as its only backdrop. Declan assumed this was the one Marlee used when she was working on her own stuff, as it mirrored the scene of almost every lecture he had attended.

The next area was a desk with two chairs behind it and a blank screen behind the chairs. It was reminiscent of a local news broadcast with chairs for two anchors. Similar to *SportsCenter*. That was where he should probably practice.

The final set was two oversized upholstered chairs with a coffee table between them and a potted silk fern behind each chair. Talk-show set. Neither of them would be spending much of their practice time there, although the chairs looked comfy. Declan thought about easing Marlee's warm body down into one of those chairs and kneeling in front of her…

He mentally shook himself to get with the program and turned to survey the rest of the studio.

Directly facing the three sets was a video camera set up on a swiveling tripod. The configuration allowed for the camera to face any of the three sets in their entirety. To the side of the camera was a large television, a laptop, and numerous cables, which Declan assumed allowed simultaneous playback of the recorded image and availability for viewing later, via downloading the file to the laptop. There was a table nearby with a bunch of extra USB cables and some unopened thumb drives.

Two metal folding chairs were near the wall by the door. Against the other wall were a few long, banquet-style tables that held a microwave, a coffeepot, some packaged condiments and creamers, Styrofoam coffee cups, and Marlee's leather satchel, her notebook and a pen lying beside it.

Pretty sparse, but then you didn't want a lot of distractions when you were going to be rehearsing and recording. Declan figured being in the same small room with Marlee was distraction enough.

He took off his jacket and threw it on one of the folding chairs. Marlee had hung her long camel hair coat on a coat rack in a corner, and Declan saw dripping boots placed on the floor underneath. Alongside the boots were mittens with melting snow and a knit wool hat. Declan turned to look at Marlee and saw her sensible—but designer—pumps that now adorned her slender feet. She was on the newscasters' set, leaning against the desk, hands clasped at hip level, her eyes following Declan.

"Did you walk here? In this cold?" Declan asked.

"Yes, and yes, it was very cold—I didn't realize how cold, or I probably would have driven."

"Do you walk to campus every day?"

"No, sometimes in the fall and spring, but never in the winter."

"Then why today?" Declan thought he knew the answer even though he was sure that Marlee wouldn't admit it. He had felt the same pent-up sexual energy coursing through his body this morning. He'd gotten only a few hours' sleep, but the zing of knowing he'd see Marlee again had him humming.

He knew his body well—it was his instrument for doing his job, and he would normally enjoy an extensive workout to expend this sexual hunger. But he didn't need to work out anymore, he remembered, and the pang that he'd felt when he first woke up this morning returned once again.

He didn't have to work out again, or monitor his protein levels during the week so he'd peak on Sundays, or watch hours of videotape in the tiny viewing room at the Pumas'

Complex that was known as Tate's Mansion because of all the time he spent there, or any of that bullshit.

Trouble was, he had a suspicion that he'd miss that bullshit more than he was willing to admit. It was really all he'd known, all he had ever done, from Pop Warner football in fifth grade to yesterday afternoon.

He wasn't sure he was capable of gracefully handling what the future would bring. Damn, but he didn't want to be one of those guys who retired, opened a restaurant, and sat around entertaining the diners while explaining the delicacies of evading Joey Robinson in the Super Bowl.

This broadcasting thing was his shot. A way to stay involved with football, the game he lived and breathed, while still maintaining his dignity. He had to get this gig, and that meant getting comfortable in front of a camera.

"I felt like the exercise this morning," Marlee said. She hesitated, then, as if deciding to lay her cards on the table, she raised her chin, looked him in the eye, and continued, "I didn't get much sleep last night, and woke up feeling, um… unsatisfied…so I decided to walk here and clear out the cobwebs, both mentally and physically."

Boy, she didn't play games, did she? He liked that about her. It was his style as well. Most of the women Declan came in contact with played all sorts of games—first to get his attention, then to get him into bed, then to keep him in their lives. Declan went along with some, but declined to play most of the women's games.

"*You* were unsatisfied? Darlin', I could tell you a thing or two about waking up unsatisfied," he said.

"I wasn't the one who ended the evening. *Darlin'.*"

"There's no way I would have left last night if I didn't have to."

"Was it some type of emergency? Is everything okay? Should you even be here this morning?"

Answering her questions in the same rapid-fire delivery, he said, "Yes. Sort of; at least it's under control. And the entire Denver Broncos defensive line couldn't have kept me from seeing you this morning." Declan moved to the set, stepped onto the platform, and leaned against the desk as well. He shifted his weight to one hip and turned to face Marlee as she did the same. "The call last night was from my agent, who was still at the party. There was a fire at my house last night."

"Declan, oh my God, why didn't you say something sooner? Was anyone hurt? Is it burned to the ground? God, I feel like such a shrew trying to make you feel guilty for leaving last night." She placed her hand on his arm, and her whole body turned into him.

He placed his hand over hers and began to stroke her long fingers. "You weren't a shrew, you were disappointed. So was I. The fire was small, thank God, and nobody was hurt. Someone in the kitchen put a dishtowel too near one of those Bunsen burner things that the caterers used. The kitchen is a wreck, and there's some smoke damage throughout the downstairs, but nothing on the second floor. The party had mostly cleared out by then. Apparently some of the guys were on a mission to find me and had left to go in search of all my usual haunts. The catering staff, my agent, a couple of players, and some, um, women were all that were left. By the time I got there, everything was under control. All I could do was call the insurance company, get some stuff for the next few days, and go to a hotel."

"You went to a hotel alone after that ordeal?"

He didn't think it wise to mention the offers he'd had for beds from the women still at the party. His agent was only in town for Declan's last game, and staying at a hotel himself.

Declan reached for Marlee's hand. "Yes, I went to a hotel. Alone. It was four in the morning, my house was a wreck, I had nowhere to go for the next few nights, and the one woman I wanted was home alone in her bed without me."

It had been an overwhelming day on all accounts. His last game as a professional athlete, a loss—which Declan never easily put from his mind in all the years he had played—meeting Marlee, and the fire. Yet it was thoughts of Marlee that kept him from falling asleep for several hours after he'd checked into a Brookline hotel. She was so different from most of the women he knew, and yet something about her seemed so comfortable, so familiar.

"I'm so sorry. What a horrible thing to have happen."

"Thanks. Like I said, I'm just thankful nobody was hurt. The damage could have been a lot worse. Actually, if it had to happen, the timing of it was pretty good. I'm meeting this week with the insurance people, the contractors, and the cleaning crews, and then next week, while I'm in New York, they'll be able to do most of the repairs. It should be all ready by the time I'm back."

"But you won't be living there much longer, will you? I mean, you'll be moving to New York, right?"

Declan had thought that scenario through several times. It hinged, of course, on him being offered something from the networks. "I've decided to keep my house. I really like it, I've been in it nearly six years, and I've put a lot of work into it to get it just the way I want it. I'll get an apartment in New York, or Connecticut if I get on with ESPN. I'll be traveling a ton anyway, so I might as well have a home base here, right in the good ol' Beantown. I can be at Logan in forty-five minutes on a good day, with all the lights in my favor."

"I don't blame you, it's a great house. And though I only saw a small part of it, I really liked it. It reminded me of mine

—on a much larger scale, of course. But kind of what I'd do with my dream house if I had an NFL salary."

"Thanks. I'd like to say you'll get to see every square inch of it, especially all four bedrooms"—Declan gave her a devilish smile—"but it's not going to be up to visitors for some time now."

What neither of them said, but both of them thought, was that by the time Declan's home was again presentable, they would have gone their separate ways.

"Right. To work, then."

By mutual agreement, they both parted and went to their respective corners.

Chapter 6

An easy flow between them came for the rest of the morning and into the afternoon. Marlee ran through her entire lecture while Declan watched, wrote notes, and, she surmised, feigned interest in a subject that couldn't possibly hold any interest to him.

After she was done, they rotated the large TV so they could sit in the comfortable talk-show set chairs and watch the playback. They turned the chairs so that they both faced the TV. Declan moved his chair so that he was close enough for their legs to touch.

She paused the tape at each point where she wanted to relate what she was saying to football. Declan would give her an idea and she'd mark it in her notes. He had some very good ideas, and she was a bit unsettled at his grasp of the content. She had toned it down a little due to her upcoming new audience's lack of expertise, but, as it stood now, until she did more editing, it was still pretty heady stuff, with lots of statistics.

Declan became excited and was incredibly helpful when Marlee gave him her itinerary of scheduled lectures. "Duke is your first stop? Duke in mid-January? Marlee, you've got to talk about basketball there, not football."

"I know even less about basketball than I do football." As Declan brushed aside her objection with a swift wave of his hand, she continued, "You don't seem to understand. If I go in and make a mockery of my speech by adding too much sports talk, and it's obvious that I know nothing about it, it will highly negate my credibility. And I need that credibility to help get some good funding passed."

Declan ignored Marlee and said, "Look, I'll write it all out tonight, the basketball phraseology as compared to the football. Then I'll mark on your itinerary which stops you should use the football and which ones the basketball, okay? It'll be fine, Marlee. Look at how quickly you picked up the football stuff. We have it interspersed cleanly throughout your lecture; all you need to do is practice it a few times, then learn the basketball parts and get those down. Piece of cake."

Marlee knew it would be. She had great memorization ability, and it had served her well whenever she had to do a lecture circuit. She had her speeches on cards and written out long-hand, and, of course, a visual presentation to go with it, but she seldom glanced at anything when she spoke. She was, after all, an expert on public speaking.

She would just simply become as familiar with the football and basketball jargon, and the incorporations would be flawless. Today was only Monday, she had the rest of the week to work on it. And to work with Declan, she reminded herself.

Thank goodness she was so polished at public speaking. Being in a small room with Declan after he had bestowed that passionate kiss upon her was more distracting than a room of two thousand people. It had taken several minutes for her heart rate to return to normal and her body to stop aching.

She had covered by taking an inordinate amount of time setting up the video equipment and the podium stage.

"Thank you. I really do appreciate your help with this. I know it'll be much better than if I just threw in some football terms." She was disappointed that he had said he'd work on it tonight. She had hoped that maybe they'd be spending the evening together.

"You're welcome. Listen, I know it's early for dinner, but we skipped lunch and I'm starving. Let me take you out somewhere. I'd love to cook for you, Marlee, but my kitchen…"

Marlee could almost see a wince as he remembered the current state of his home.

"Do you cook often?" Marlee couldn't wrap her mind around the vision of big, bad football player Declan in a kitchen.

"All the time. I love to cook. I had my kitchen specially designed. It was great."

She smiled at him, picturing him in the kitchen. He smiled back, and then his gaze dropped to her mouth. Remembering their earlier kiss, she licked her lips.

He let out a low growl, then said, "Come on, I need something to eat, and I need to get my hands on you." Having near the same thoughts herself, she quickly headed for the coat rack and began throwing her notes into her satchel.

They had a fast bite to eat at a diner just off campus, one of her favorite places to pick up something on her way home when she didn't feel like cooking.

She was amazed at how many times Declan was interrupted for autographs. She knew he was a star athlete, but had not put it in everyday terms before. Young Boston College coeds openly propositioned him, and to Marlee's delight he politely brushed them all off.

Marlee was stunned to realize one of the girls was a student who had four-pointed her theory of speech course last year. Marlee had assumed that the studious girl had a better head on her shoulders than to openly make a pass at a man she didn't know. But then, was Marlee any better? She quickly let that thought drop from her mind. Declan had made the pass at her, right? She was merely responding in kind. *Right, girlfriend, tell yourself another!*

Every time they had more than a few minutes of uninterrupted time, Declan would turn the talk to their immediate, and incredibly strong, attraction for each other. He was as blunt as he had been the previous night, telling her how attracted to her he was. He found the subject curious and wanted to deeply explore it. The topic flustered Marlee, but if she was honest with herself—and she had decided that throughout this little fling she would need to be honest with herself or risk being hurt—she was also very aroused. Declan's casual comments of what he'd envisioned them doing earlier, as she stood behind the podium, seeped into her body, making it both languid and tense.

"I know it's the speaker who is supposed to envision the audience in their underwear, but darlin', it was definitely the other way around today."

"Don't laugh, I've used that technique." She was trying to deflect the subject, but Declan wouldn't allow it.

"Maybe it has something to do with yesterday being my last game, how uncertain my future is, and how stable and secure you seem to be. I don't know. I really don't want to analyze it to death, Marlee, I just know that I want you. Badly." As Marlee opened her mouth to comment on that, Declan cut her off. "And I know when attraction is mutual, so don't deny what we've got going on, you're hot for me too."

"You're preaching to the choir, Declan." Marlee ducked her

head to avoid Declan's impaling gaze as she confessed her mutual desire.

"So, you agree there's this incredible chemistry between us? You seemed to go back and forth last night."

"My perception on the subject did fluctuate enormously last night."

"There you go again with the big words. Marlee, can you just say that you want my bod?"

"I want your bod."

"Check, please."

THEY WERE SILENT AS HE DROVE THEM TO HER HOUSE, except for the few times Marlee needed to speak to give him directions. Declan didn't speak for a couple of reasons.

He didn't want to break the hypnotic spell they both seemed to be under since she'd told him she wanted him. He knew it, of course. Could tell from the sparks that had flown between them since they first shook hands at Joey's introduction. It still felt great to hear her say it. Declan's cock had leapt to attention at her pronouncement. And hadn't subsided one little bit.

The other reason he didn't speak was that he didn't want Marlee to change her mind. He knew this was something new for her, being with a man like Declan. At least he thought it was. He wasn't naive enough to know that a woman who looked like she did and was as confident as she was wouldn't have a bevy of suitors around. But he envisioned them all as pipe-smoking, elbow-patched, jacket-wearing intellectuals. Not someone who would encourage Marlee to engage the tigress Declan was now certain she was capable of becoming.

And yet she was still single, and seemingly not involved

with anyone. Whatever the reason for that, Marlee was unattached right now and he was going to take advantage.

He thought if there was conversation in the car, not only might the spell break, but she might just talk herself out of it again. Declan couldn't bear the thought of not getting to finally touch Marlee, so he kept his mouth shut and drove.

Fast.

MARLEE HAD NO INTENTION OF BACKING OUT, BUT SHE didn't want to talk too much about it, either.

She wanted Declan. She wanted whatever time she could get with him, even if it was only for the week.

Who was she kidding? She wanted him *because* it would only be for a week. Anything more would be a disaster. They were too different, and she didn't want to waste time pursuing something that had no shot of survival.

Not again.

But for now…the idea of Declan alone, naked, with that glorious body exposed for her inspection and pleasure…

The thought alone made Marlee shiver.

At her final direction, Declan turned into her driveway and turned off the engine. She tried to see the house and area as he might. It was a nice, quiet street, lined with older homes that had been lovingly kept up. Besides being close to work, she adored the Chestnut Hill area, and her smaller home.

"Nice neighborhood."

"Thanks."

He went around and opened the door for her. He took her hand as they walked up the shoveled sidewalk to the front door. She tried to keep her pulse calm and steady, praying he wouldn't feel her excitement through the clasp of her hand.

She dug her keys out of her bag and turned her back to

Declan as she placed it in the lock. He placed his hands on her waist as she tried to unlock her front door. Her movements were jerky and tense, and it took her a couple of tries to get the dang thing unlocked.

"Nice house," he murmured into her neck as he gently kissed the soft skin just below her ear.

"Thanks."

Finally getting the door open, she waved him through, then entered herself. She turned back to the door to lock it and put the safety chain on. She turned on the light switch, but while her hand was still on it, Declan placed his hand over hers and turned it back off. He slid her bag off her shoulder and let it drop to the floor, causing a heavy thump that didn't seem nearly as loud as the beating of her heart. He plucked the keys from her hand and they plinked as they fell to the floor. He placed her hands on the door, above her head, almost as if he were a cop and was making her assume the position.

She'd assume any position he wanted, and maybe even a few she'd think up.

He placed his hands on top of hers, then slid them down her arms, as if checking for weapons. She felt *his* weapon as he pressed his hard arousal into her back. He put her hands down to her sides for only a moment so he could slide her coat and then her suit jacket off, which he promptly threw aside. He then put her arms back on the door, and slid his hands down them again. This time when he reached her shoulders, he swept to the front of her silk blouse.

"Nice room."

"Thanks."

Marlee knew Declan hadn't seen one iota of her house before he'd turned the lights out, but she acknowledged the compliment all the same. His hands felt amazing on her body as he started to undo the buttons of her blouse. He untucked it from her slacks to get the last two buttons undone. She was so anxious she almost ripped the thing apart herself. Marlee expected him to put her arms down again to get the blouse off, but he didn't. Instead, he placed one hand across her tummy and the other across her breastbone and kissed her neck.

Finally, to feel his touch on her skin. Ever since their kiss this morning, it seemed like she'd been waiting an eternity to feel that connection.

No. Not an eternity. The thought once again drove home to her that she'd only known this man a little more than a day. She chose not to think of that, but to concentrate on his kisses that were so warm and soft on her neck. He moved up and kissed her earlobe, gently sucking it into his mouth.

"Nice neck."

He returned his attentions to her neck, which was barely holding up her spinning head.

"Thanks."

She arched her back just a little. Just enough to give him better access to her neck and to also grind her behind into his erection. He let out a small groan and moved his hand up to cup one of her breasts, prompting Marlee to exhale a groan of her own.

He cupped a breast fully. She was busty and spilled over his hands. Declan kneaded the breast, and his other hand, joining in the fun, cupped her other breast. Always such a sensitive place for her, they firmed and hardened at his touch. His fingers brushed over her front clasp and stilled, as if finding treasure. One sure flick of his fingers and he had her unsnapped. As if being set free after a long incarceration, her breasts willingly fell into his waiting grasp. She let out a sigh of pleasure, and relief to finally be touched like this by him.

He took his hands away from her breasts for only a second. He put his thumb and index finger from each hand just inside her mouth. She gently sucked in his digits, making them wet. He took them away and returned them to her now bared breasts. Her breath quickened as his wet fingers sought out her already hard nipples. As he rolled them between his thumbs and forefingers, Marlee gasped and ground herself into him again. This time he was ready for her, and did some grinding of his own.

"Nice tits."

"Thanks."

He was squeezing the nipples now, pulling them out, mimicking a suckling motion with his hands. His mouth was still hot on her neck, sucking there. She knew he was probably leaving a mark. Part of her loved the thought of that. Of being branded by Declan.

His chest was molded to her back, as if he was trying to get as close to her as possible. Which was A-okay with her. Through the fog in her brain, she could hear his breathing become labored, which seemed to propel her own desire higher. She pushed back into him, and he began stroking himself against her backside.

Marlee gasped. Declan moved his hand from her breast and down her stomach. Undoing the button and zipper of Marlee's slacks, he guided his hand downward. He nudged aside her satin panties. She knew the silky material was wet with her arousal. He eased his fingers down to cover her.

"Nice mound."

He touched her coarse hair and then slipped his fingers inside her folds. God, she was so wet for him. And he seemed to be feeling the same intensity that was coursing through her body.

"Thanks."

Marlee could barely get the lone word out. She knew she was close. The way Declan touched her…His fingers continued to circle her nub. Her hands, that had been only resting on the door, now braced her weight, and she used the leverage to press back into him. She leaned her neck back, now able to take in Declan's scent as he nuzzled forward, to the front of her neck.

He smelled like man. No other way to describe it. Pure, strong, virile, aroused man.

His tongue ran along her neck, imitating the soft, circular symphony that his fingers played out below. She felt the softness of something else as well, and her fuddled mind realized it was the yellow scarf. That raggedy-ass scarf, that was so out of place on the polished hunk, was softer than any fabric Marlee had ever felt on her skin before. It was an incredible contrast to the rough texture of Declan's tongue and his callused fingers.

He slipped one inside her, gliding it in easily due to her wetness. With his thumb, he continued to stroke her, circling her pulsating clit. He picked up speed with his thumb while he edged another finger inside her, then pressed up with both fingers while he scraped his thumbnail across her.

That was all it took. Marlee's entire body stiffened, then began convulsing. His right hand, which had seemed permanently attached to her breast, lowered, and he held her tightly around the waist as his left hand continued administering the touch that was taking her over the edge.

She bucked back against him, her head thrown back. She heard several of her hairpins fall to the floor as he guided her through her climax. Portions of her hair fell down her back and over Declan's brow as he sucked on her neck. Her trembling continued as he deftly worked his magic on her body.

She'd never had such an intense orgasm; it seemed to go on and on. Her eyes closed, flashes of white lights passed before her and the term "saw fireworks" briefly ran through her mind. Ragged exhales escaped her lips, and then she sucked in a huge breath as another wave was upon her. She silently prayed for Declan to take away his hand lest she pass out, but she also wished that he would never stop rubbing her there. And there. And also there.

He lifted his fingers inside Marlee one last time and then eased them out. He drew his thumb away from her as well, and raised his hand to join his other one, clasping them both around Marlee's waist.

One last surge of pleasure wafted through Marlee, and then slowly, so slowly, her breathing began to return to normal. Her heartbeat, which had surpassed erratic, once again became a strong *thump-thump*. Happy that Declan was for all intents holding her up at the waist because her legs had become limp, she leaned forward and slumped her head on top of her hands, resting her upper body weight against her front door.

Declan waited another moment, as if making sure Marlee was all the way down after her exhilarating high. He then turned her around to face him. Pushing back the hair that had come undone, gently tucking it behind her ears, he leaned forward, kissed her gently on her forehead, and tilted her chin up so that she looked straight at him.

"Nice orgasm."

"Thanks."

She wanted to say more than the simple word. She wanted to get down on her knees and kiss the ground he walked on for giving her such an intense gift. She wanted to sing his praises to all who would listen about the magic of his fingers, the knowledge of his touch. All she could manage was thanks.

Declan smiled at her. Not his trademark killer cat-that-ate-the-canary smile, but a soft grin, something Marlee had not seen from him before now.

He squatted down so that his shoulder was even with Marlee's waist. He reached up behind Marlee and pushed her down at her middle, causing her to bend over Declan's incredibly broad shoulder. He came up fast, taking her with him, her feet dangling until he reached an arm around and anchored her to him by holding the back of her knees and placing his other hand across her fanny.

The rush of blood to her head was quick and strong, but not as exhilarating as what had just happened to her.

"Now," he said, "which way to the bedroom and I'll show you some ways you can have *me* saying thanks."

Chapter 7

Marlee was lean, but a substantial woman, though she felt light as a feather in Declan's excited arms. He carried her toward the stairs that he could see with the help of the streetlights shining dimly through the windows of her living room. He took the stairs nearly two at a time, now oblivious to Marlee's encumbrance.

Sounding as impatient as Declan felt, she guided him to her bedroom. "Straight ahead, last door." Declan made a beeline and turned on the wall switch as he entered the room.

The room was just what Declan expected from the—albeit limited—time he'd spent with Marlee. It was warm and cozy; there was a large cherry sleigh bed with a comforter set in a design of deep greens and maroons. The dresser and tables were of the same dark cherry wood. There were picture frames on the dresser and womanly things: bottles of perfume, brushes, what looked to be an antique jewelry box.

Books were stacked next to the nightstand on the right side of the bed. Declan felt a moment of glee when he saw no books on the left side. There was no man that was here on a regular enough basis to have books on the nightstand. Declan didn't read too much into that, but he did like the thought. A brief vision of the novel he was currently reading lying on that table went through his mind. Yeah, it would look good on cherry.

A large walk-in closet on the right side of the room, and a door that he assumed led to the master bath on the left. Together, it all took up the entire width of the house. Declan liked it. The whole room was neat and orderly, but didn't scream anal-retentive. Just like Marlee—neat, orderly, but approachable, comfortable. And definitely touchable.

He ran his arms down her calves and took her pumps from her feet. In their hurry to leave the studio, Marlee had left her shoes on instead of changing back to her boots. Which was good, because it would've taken a bit more balance than he had to unlace and remove Marlee's boots with her hanging over his shoulder. The pumps slid easily from her feet and dropped to the floor.

He moved his hands back up her long and shapely legs until he reached the top of her trouser socks at her knees. One by one he removed both until she was barefoot.

Declan squatted, bent slightly at the waist, and let Marlee's body slide down his until her feet touched the floor. He slowly rose up, allowing his torso to glide against Marlee's as she righted herself. The shock of the face-to-face contact sped through them both. Declan was just a little out of breath from the exertion of carrying Marlee up the stairs, and she seemed a tad dizzy from being suspended upside down. It only added to the physical sensations they both were feeling.

Marlee reached for Declan's belt, obviously wanting to reciprocate, but he held her hands and pulled them away from his body.

"Slow down, baby, we've got all night. And you've got a lot to learn."

"Excuse me?" Marlee's look was a little stung. Her body stiffened and Declan realized his mistake.

"About football, Marlee. Football. A lot to learn about football." He waited till this sank in and her stance relaxed just the smallest amount, but Declan noticed it and smiled. He was already attuned to her body. When a woman shatters in your arms with her sweet ass grinding against your hard-on, you sort of got to know her rhythms. Fast.

"We're going to talk football? Now?" She stepped back, away from Declan, deeper into the room.

"Not talk. Show. You picked that stuff up today really quickly. But now it's time to really delve into what you'll be talking about. We don't want anyone picking up on your lack of knowledge, do we?" As he said this, his eyes left Marlee's face and went to her breasts, which were still bared, her bra and blouse open and hanging at her sides.

Declan knew their size and shape, had nearly memorized it when they were against the door, but this was the first time he had seen them. They were full and large and he now knew how the euphemism "melons" came into being. He was never one for slang when talking about a woman's body, he was much more titillated by the real words, but that's what they were—ripe, heavy, firm melons.

Her nipples were a dusky rose and sizable; they were also pebbled, puckered. Declan wasn't sure if they were still hard from his touch downstairs or from the growing arousal he now saw on Marlee's face. It took an effort, but he raised his vision from her beautiful breasts and met her eyes. He knew his eyes radiated with desire; there was no way he could hide it—and didn't want to. He could feel his already hard cock stiffen even more when he saw the same desire in Marlee's gaze.

Her chin jutted out, and her shoulders squared, causing her breasts to sway. "Okay, Mr. Football Hero, show me."

"That's my girl—never step back from a challenge, do ya, baby?" He walked further into the room, slipping his leather jacket from his shoulders and draping it across a rocking chair that sat in the corner. He reached his arm over his opposite shoulder, grabbing the back of his shirt and pulling it over his head and throwing it to the floor. The yellow scarf came with it.

Marlee gasped at the sight of Declan's shoulders and chest. He could tell she didn't want to make the telltale sound, but his chest puffed out with pride that she had. She moved to him, poised to reach once again for his belt, but seemingly waiting for Declan's lead.

"Like what you see, darlin'?"

His little minx gave a nonchalant shrug. "Meh. It's okay." But she wasn't fooling anyone, least of all him.

He chuckled at her feigned indifference; he'd seen her eyes widen in appreciation when he'd taken his shirt off. Declan's grueling physical regimen was solely designed to keep him at his best on the playing field. He'd taken good care of his body, and that had allowed him to play longer than most at this level. He didn't have the size of a Joey Robinson, but he'd spent plenty of time in the weight room. The effect his body had on women was an added perk.

Marlee moved to Declan and he brushed her blouse and undone bra from her shoulders to the floor, leaving them both naked from the waist up. "Just leveling the playing field." His hands swept back up her arms after discarding the garments, and came to rest on her shoulders and neck. He stroked her lightly, loving the softness of her pale skin.

Marlee eased her neck back slowly, seeming to delight in Declan's touch. Her neck going back caused her breasts to edge forward so that they came to rest against his chest. The texture of his chest hair tickled her sensitized nipples and her breath left her in a soft hiss. Her hands came to rest on his waist, and he loved the feel of her hands on him.

He pushed her slacks down, past her slim waist, over the flared hips, along the toned thighs and legs that seemed to go on forever. Declan followed the pants path with his hands, and when they had reached the floor, he slid his hands slowly back up her calves and then her thighs, resting his hand on her hips. Her skin was so soft to the touch, with just a sniff of jasmine reaching him. There was definite muscle tone in her legs, but not the hardness of a runner. Probably yoga. It was tone, without the bulk, which, when compared with the linemen on the team, was how Declan would describe his own body.

She was only in peach satin panties, trimmed with the smallest hint of lace. Peach. It had matched the now unneeded bra. Classy, yet hot. Declan liked that. He liked it a lot.

"Then, by all means, let's keep the playing field…level," Marlee nearly whispered, her throat catching a little bit, as she undid his fly. He ached for her hands to touch his cock, but she slid his jeans down to knee level, then lifted her leg, sliding her toes up Declan's shin. When her foot reached the waistband of his jeans, she edge her toes into the fly and pushed the jeans to the floor with her foot. Her knee and outside thigh brushed against the inside of Declan's, along his boxer briefs.

He hurriedly kicked off his shoes and pulled off his socks, then stepped out of the fallen jeans. He walked her backwards until her legs came in to contact with the side of the bed. "You see, Marlee, in football, it's all about downs." He stepped back and pushed her gently at the clavicle until she fell back on to the bed, her knees dangling off the edge. Declan swiftly stepped forward and, in one smooth motion, took the back of her knees, one in each hand, and spread them apart, allowing space for him to move his body to the edge of the bed. To the edge of Marlee. The skin at the back of her knees was baby's-bottom smooth and just as soft.

"Downs?" Marlee asked as she raised her knees, her feet sliding up his legs. She placed the soles of her feet against the back of his thighs, her legs akimbo, giving Declan an open view of her. He sensed it was a bold move on her part, but he wanted to make her feel bold. Plus, she still had her panties on so she wasn't totally exposed to him. Yet.

"Yes. Downs. A team has four tries, or four downs, to move the ball ten yards. If they make it, they get another four downs for another ten yards. If they don't, the other team gets the ball and it's their turn to try." He edged forward, still standing straight, not wanting his whole body touching her. Not yet. Declan was a professional athlete and he knew about pacing himself. You wanted to have something left in the fourth quarter.

With Marlee, they could be talking about an overtime situation.

"We'll call *this* first down." He pushed his erection, clearly outlined by his briefs, into the juncture of Marlee's satin panties. The connection was exquisite pain and sounds of pleasure escaped from both of their mouths. Marlee gave a soft sigh and Declan offered up a harsh groan as he began to rub himself against her.

"First down. I get it. God, that feels good." She lifted her hips slightly so that his motion would touch more of her where she needed it. Heat poured through his body as he watched her move.

"First down always does. Feel good, that is. Getting a first down is like dodging a bullet. You always strive for a first down. The quarterback always knows where exactly on the field the first-down yard line is. Always." He rubbed against her again, creating a slow, torturous rhythm. "A good QB knows how to get to that spot."

He pulled slightly away from her and gave a self-satisfied growl when he looked down and saw a darker peach on her panties from her wetness.

"QB?"

"Quarterback."

"Oh, right. Sorry. I'm trying to grasp it all, really." With that she reached forward and tried to grasp something else as well.

"Nah unh, you don't want to get penalized for offsides, do you?" He moved just away from her reach, swatted her hand away, then moved back in.

"Offsides?"

"Moving before the ball is snapped."

"Oh, no. I definitely want to see the ball snapped." Her eyes devoured him, and his erection seemed to jerk under his shorts.

"You see, on first down, most quarterbacks will try something a little daring, because they've got three more downs, so, you know, why not go for it. But me, I figure that's what they're looking for, so I usually try something safe, a little old school, and hope for a good reaction." He leaned over her, bracing his arms on either side of her shoulders, and with no warning, took a taut nipple in his mouth and began to suckle her.

Marlee nearly leapt off the bed, and her arched back did clear the comforter. As though she couldn't handle the erotic sight, she closed her eyes and put her head back and listened to his hard sucking noises. He noticed she liked to listen to him, responded to his voice, his commands. That was good, 'cause he sure had some commands he wanted to give her.

She brought her hands up and buried them in his hair,

combing her fingers through his mane. She held his head, pulling him closer to her breasts, which was nearly impossible as Declan was already as close to her as he could get. Except he felt like he could never be too close to Marlee.

His head moved over to her other breast and this time he teased the nipple with his tongue, laving the breast completely, before he took it in his mouth and continued sucking.

Bolts of electricity flowed through them both, and she ground her panties into Declan, seeming to desperately wish the cloth barriers would disappear. He was totally with her in that desire.

Needing to feel her flesh, Declan's arms moved from the bed to Marlee, skimming her sides, playing with her breasts, circling her tummy and then dipping his fingers into the waistband of her panties. He reluctantly took his mouth from her and straightened up, standing above her. The despair of leaving those incredible breasts was quickly replaced with pure lust as he looked down at Marlee.

She looked dazed. Her elegant neck was arched, and her hair, coming undone and in disarray, was tangled about her head, the auburn waves spread out over the maroons and greens of the comforter. Her breasts, reddened and glistening from Declan's mouth, rose with her excited breathing. The pale alabaster skin now had a blush across it, reaching all the way up to her face.

And that face. Marlee's face. Declan felt a wave of possession just seeing the way she looked up at him. As if he were the only man who had ever made her feel like this. As if he was the only man who could give her what she so needed. Feelings that were too intense to identify raced through him, but he brushed them aside. He'd think about them later. Right now, he had to satisfy Marlee. Instinctively, he knew that to satisfy Marlee would satisfy himself as well.

"If your play on first down works—" Declan began.

"Oh, it definitely worked." Her hands went to her breasts, feeling the moistness Declan had left. She fingered her nipples, mimicking his motions when they'd been downstairs. The sight of her touching herself where his mouth had just been turned Declan on even more, though he would have sworn that was impossible to do.

"Good. If first down works, then you usually have three or four yards left to get, and you have a choice. To be conservative and run something small to get the yards, or say, 'Screw it, we can get those on third down, let's try something to get their attention now.'"

"And what do you do?"

His hands were just inside her panties, one at each hip. "Darlin', I like to get people's attention."

He curled his fingers around the material and, in one quick motion, ripped Marlee's panties from her, the satin making a loud tearing sound. He took the shredded panties and raised them in his right hand to his face. While his eyes locked on to her green-gold ones, he put the panties to his nose and inhaled deeply. "Mmmm. Baby, you smell wonderful. Jasmine, satin and…Marlee. I can tell how excited you are from these. How much you want me. You do want me, don't you, Marlee?"

"Y…y…yes." She was trembling now. The boldness of his words and actions had stunned her. And aroused her. He could tell she was surprised herself at how much she responded to it.

Still holding her panties to his face, he stepped out of her legs, unwrapping her from around him. He took a few quick strides to where his jeans were lying on the floor, picked them up, and grabbed his wallet out of his back pocket. He pulled a condom out of it and dropped the wallet and jeans back to the floor. He was back in the circle of Marlee's legs in an instant, and dropped the condom beside her on the bed.

"I think second down was successful." Declan smiled down at her.

"Very. You got my attention."

"That's the idea, but for the sake of your education, let's say it didn't work. That we got sacked."

"Sacked?" It was obvious she didn't know what that was, but her eyes shot to Declan's groin, to the only sack she was interested in right now. His.

Following her gaze, he chuckled. "Sacked is when the quarterback is tackled behind the line of scrimmage." At Marlee's confused look, he clarified, "From behind the spot where he started. Moving them backwards."

The look of comprehension shone in Marlee's eyes. He wasn't surprised she was catching on so quickly, even as distracted as they were. The woman had a mind that made her body seem average in comparison. And her body was anything but average. Declan couldn't ever remember being this eager to get inside a woman, and that made him want to drag it out even more.

"Okay, so you're sacked. Or I guess *I'm* sacked. Whatever. What play do you call now, coach?" She was running her legs up against the back of his thighs. It allowed Declan a full view of Marlee. Her pussy lips were slightly spread, tender and swollen, engorged from his previous touches. Declan let his hands drift softly over them, parting them. She gasped in pleasure. He broke away from her and removed his briefs, needing to have no barriers from her.

"Declan." It was more of a soft sigh than a spoken word, and the sound made his hard cock jerk. She began to ever so slightly rock her hips.

Declan saw the appreciation in Marlee's eyes as he stood

before her. He knew he was well endowed. He'd spent his life showering with other men—you tended to notice those things. And if you didn't, others did, and let you know about it.

He'd gotten similar looks from other women, but theirs were more of a self-satisfied look; like the size of Declan's dick was a direct correlation of his desire for them. It wasn't. He got the same erection for any woman he was fucking.

Or so he'd thought.

It had never seemed this intense before. Had he ever physically felt the blood rush through the veins of his cock with such clarity before? Had any woman's gaze at his naked body given him such pleasure? He didn't think so. There were a lot of firsts for him with Marlee, which, after all these years, and all the women, was a definite treat.

His fingers moved back to her center, lightly teasing, She was slick, wet, hot for him. He did this to her. He had another flash of possession. *He* did this to her. Declan made Marlee this wet, had her rolling her hips, moving herself forward, wanting his fingers to go further.

She edged closer to him, though her bottom was at the end of the mattress, and Declan brought his erection close, guiding it with one hand while he spread her lips wide with the other. He stroked himself against Marlee's tight clit, circling it with his swollen head. The sensation was delicious.

"Right. We've been sacked. That brings up, let's say, third and seven. The only option now is for a short pass to pick up the first down."

"So you're going to make a pass? Funny, I thought that had already happened." Her voice was soft and low, more husky than before, and Declan realized she was as close as he was. He could hear it in her voice, smell her arousal, certainly felt how close she was with his hand. He couldn't bear to take his fingers away from her, not when she felt so good.

"Put the condom on me, Marlee, I have my hands full." He eased back just an inch or two to allow Marlee access to his erection. She picked up the package and, with hands trembling with desire, and with Declan fingering her, tore open the package and rolled the condom onto his hard cock. He brushed her hands away from him then, not allowing her to touch him any longer than necessary. It would definitely make him go offsides.

"Touch your breasts, again, Marlee. I love to watch you touch yourself there."

Marlee didn't hesitate, and he loved that about her. She pinched her nipples and pulled on them, as Declan had done to her with his mouth. His eyes shone his approval. "That's it, baby. Sometimes a little unnecessary roughness is just what's needed to let the opponent know where you stand." She moaned in agreement, the back of her head pressing into the mattress.

"So, third down. I throw a short screen pass to a runner and hope he can pick up the extra yards with a move or two."

"A move or two?"

His hand spread her wider, and he laid his cock against her throbbing core. Set it on her, almost balancing it there, freeing that hand so that he could put a finger inside her. "You know, nothing fancy, just a move, a dance, a juke, to get the desired results." His finger slipped inside, and he swiftly added another. They went in easily, she was so slick and wet. And hot. So, so hot.

His thumb eased up under his shaft and made tiny circles around her nub. It was distended and tender. He flicked over it, but realized from Marlee's intake of breath how sensitive it was. He instead began stroking the surrounding flesh. Declan

could feel the vibrations pouring from her. Her head began to
roll from side to side. Gorgeous, naked, his fingers inside her,
his cock resting on her, his thumb practicing magic within her.
He was reeling with sensation just watching her. Her own
hands were on her breasts where he'd wanted them, where his
eyes were now watched.

Her breath came in short gasps and her beautiful face went
into full flush.

"That's it, Marlee. Get there. Get there, baby. Get your
first down." His fingers inside her wiggled upwards, scraping
the tender skin, and his thumb once again flicked across her.
"Come for me, Marlee."

His voice sent her over. "Oh, God. Declan." Her body
stiffened, then burst. She convulsed around his fingers as her
body cried out. Her breasts jiggled as she gasped for breath.
Declan coaxed her body along with soft whispers of
encouragement and with slow pressure from his hands. He was
taking all he could from her, not letting her come down until
he was ready. She heaved again, spiraling higher than she had
the first time.

After what seemed a breathtaking eternity, Declan slowed
his touch to a soft stroking, and Marlee began her descent.
Her breathing returned to normal and she seemed to regain
her focus, which she then turned on Declan.

"So, the moves were made and the desired effect was
achieved," she said when she finally spoke. She bent at the
waist to sit up, but he moved a hand to her tummy and gently
held her down.

"Yes, but let's say, again for the sake of your education,
that the pass was incomplete."

"You threw a bad pass? Do you do that?" she teased.

"No. Never. Any pass of mine that wasn't caught was
entirely the receiver's fault." They shared a smile at his teasing.

Holy shit, she'd just come apart in his hands and that smile—her smile—made him even harder.

He moved his hands to the tops of her thighs, caressing, stroking. His erection was tight up against her, hovering near her entrance. "Right. So, fourth down. This is when you'd normally punt it away, so the other team has further to go. But if it's only a few yards, sometimes you go for it."

"And are we? Going to go for it, I mean?" It wasn't a loaded question, but Declan felt there might be all sorts of deeper meanings in that simple ask. He seriously wanted to… go for it. With Marlee.

"Absolutely." He skimmed his hands down her thighs; when he got to her knees he bent them, causing her to take her calves from behind him, where they'd been locked to his thighs. Though he mourned the loss of contact, he had something better in mind and Marlee saw it from the gleam in his eyes as they locked on hers.

"So. Let's say fourth and two, that's when you'd typically go for it. This is easy, a quarterback sneak, where I take the ball and dive through the line. Or hand off to a bruiser of a running back and let him bulldoze his way through. Pretty standard stuff." He lifted her knees, ran his hands down her calves, and placed her feet over his shoulders. At her look of surprise, he continued, "Except…"

"Except?"

Still standing, he spread his legs a little, giving himself better leverage.

"Except I hate standard stuff. So, instead of the short run, I call something different. Something I'm really good at, something I love to do."

"What's that?"

Declan took one hand from Marlee's thigh and guided

himself inside her wet sheath, totally immersing himself in one hard stroke.

"I go deep."

And he did.

Did Marlee's gasp drown out Declan's groan or was it the other way around? He didn't know, and didn't care, so great was the sensation of being buried—finally—in Marlee. He only allowed himself a second to bask in the warmth before he began to move. Long, deep strokes that made her hands leave her breasts and go to her mouth and eyes, like her senses were overwhelmed. He knew his were.

Declan's hands left her thighs and grabbed her waist, anchoring her as he pounded into her, his rhythm picking up speed and intensity. He could feel his balls slapping into her ass as she lifted herself into him, meeting his thrusts.

Knowing she was again close, he forced her to look into his eyes. They were shining. With passion? Desire? Something else? All of the above? Declan wasn't sure, and, really, he didn't care. His eyes were on hers and he was about to come inside her. Come with her. His strokes became shorter, fiercer.

"Look at us, Marlee—look at where I'm inside you. Look at how well we fit together. Watch me come, Marlee. Watch me come inside you." She followed his eyes as they lowered to where their bodies joined, and once again, it was his words that sent her over.

Her body spiraled as it had before, and her body shook, but it felt deeper, more connected. It was connected—literally. To him. His shudders as he reached his release caused a soft smile from her, which he barely registered.

Buried deep in Marlee was one of the best feelings he'd ever had. Right up there with winning the Rose Bowl and the Super Bowl. Maybe even better, because Marlee wasn't going anywhere, while his playing days had always been finite. He could achieve this…this…whatever it was with Marlee indefinitely.

Had he had any energy left, Declan would have jumped at the unsettling thought. But he didn't. What strength he did have was spent scooting Marlee and himself to the middle of the bed so that he could touch all of her body. Careful not to leave her, he arranged them on their sides, Declan still buried inside her, her thigh thrown over his. He wrapped his arms around her, and for the first time since this morning at the studio, kissed her mouth. It was warm and soft and she kissed him back. She broke away, looked at him, then leaned over to whisper in his ear.

"Touchdown."

Chapter 8

E ven though several hours of lovemaking had passed, it was only ten o'clock in the evening and Declan was hungry. They'd had a very early dinner at the diner, and they had more than worked off the small Greek salads they'd consumed. He supposed it would take a while for his body's metabolism to come down from his heavy, workout-based existence. He'd have to be careful.

Declan loved to cook, and eat, and was good at both. Without the daily weightlifting sessions and practice, he'd probably get a gut, and then some. The thought of love handles made him mentally shudder. Never one for vanity, Declan still acknowledged that turning to fat would kill him. Plus, if this broadcasting thing worked out, he'd have to watch his weight. He grinned. Just another reminder that he had now joined the everyday ranks—paying attention to his figure.

He slipped out of bed and into his jeans, leaving them unbuttoned and slung low on his hips. An exhausted Marlee barely noticed his movements, and made none of her own. His clothes were scattered all over her bedroom floor where they had been discarded. After some searching, he found his shirt and threw it at her. "Here, throw this on, and let's raid your fridge." Marlee's head perked up instantly and she began finding the sleeves of Declan's shirt.

"Oh sure, I leave your bed after satisfying you for hours and you don't even look up. But the first mention of food, and you're scrambling to get dressed," he teased. Although, if he were honest, it had stung the smallest amount when Marlee hadn't reached for him when he'd risen.

Declan had gotten out of a lot of beds, and that had never happened before. Normally the woman would be in his arms like a shot, kissing and caressing, reaching for his dick to try to get him to stay. Just another way Marlee was different.

"Priorities. It's all about priorities," Marlee shot back as she breezed past him. On her way to the door she stopped and reached to the floor for something, unknowingly giving Declan an eyeful as the shirt slid up her long thighs and revealed just the beginnings of her heart-shaped ass. She came up with the retrieved item—his scarf—slung it around her neck, flipped the excess around her shoulders like an old-time daredevil pilot, and proceeded out the bedroom door.

The sight of Marlee, long hair finally totally unbound and disheveled from their escapades, wearing only his shirt and scarf, made Declan harden again. The idea of Marlee wearing *only* the scarf about sent him through the roof.

His stomach growled, and for a moment Declan couldn't decide which of his basic needs he would satisfy first. He followed her downstairs.

The lights had been out when Declan had carried Marlee upstairs. She'd now turned them on so they could find their way to the kitchen. Declan was shocked at Marlee's living room decor. It was nearly a mirror image of his own. It was smaller, more modest, but the same layout, the same style, the same obvious care had gone into her choices as had his.

It was a country/contemporary look. It had warm, soft, oversized furniture that was certainly passable for formal entertaining, but was meant to be used by a family. Comfort being the main goal. A chair and a half with a large ottoman, an inviting sofa, a wooden rocker with a chenille throw lying over one of its arms.

One of the walls was painted a deep, dramatic color that Declan figured had some fancy name, but looked like a deep pink or light red to him. It was eye-catching, and was something he had tried in his home, only with a different color. He liked the way Marlee's had turned out better. The textures were warm cottons and chenilles, deep, rich colors that made the room seem welcoming instead of formal. The fireplace was the focal point of the room, just as Declan had designed his.

He walked to the fireplace, drawn to the family photos displayed on the mantel. He had done the same thing at his place. Marlee had used wooden frames, all different, for her photos, while Declan had gone the same route, but with silver frames.

Marlee joined him. "I know, I know…it should be a gas fireplace. I thought about converting it. I know the sell… they're cleaner, less mess, more heat, controllable, but…"

"It's just not the same as burning wood," Declan finished. "I feel the same way. I went round and round with the contractor over mine, but I was adamant. I wanted a real one. Plus, I love to chop my own wood every spring. It's great for keeping my throwing shoulder loose during the off-season." He pointed to the mantel. "I like what you've done with the pictures. I kind of tried the same thing. Problem is, my nieces and nephews grow so fast, it's almost impossible to keep the damned things updated."

Marlee chuckled. "I know what you mean. See him?"

Declan followed her finger as she pointed to a photo of a cherubic three-year-old in a Captain Hook costume, holding what was undoubtedly a trick-or-treat bag. He had Marlee's auburn hair, in a little boy's mushroom cut, and Declan leaned in closer to see the boy had Marlee's warm green-gold eyes as well.

"He's now a freshman in high school. The others are more recent; I just could never bring myself to take this one down. I'd taken him trick-or-treating that year, and he was so funny in that costume. He nearly put out my eye several times with that Styrofoam hook. When he comes over I invariably catch him trying to hide it."

"Does most of your family live in the area?" Declan realized that he knew nothing about the background of the woman in whose body he had just found incredible comfort. That was nothing new for Declan. He seldom spent more than a few dates and a couple of nights of sex with any one woman. And certainly never taking the time to find out about their family. Truth was, they weren't the type of women who Declan could envision taking their nephew trick-or-treating.

With Marlee, the thought of not knowing anything about her family bothered him. For all he knew, these kids in the pictures could have been hers. He knew they weren't. But he had gotten that information from asking Joey on the phone this morning about Marlee's marital and children status, not because he'd gotten to know Marlee all that well.

He felt as if he'd known her longer. It could have been the physical intimacy they'd just shared, but Declan felt almost a déjá vu thing with Marlee. Had felt it even before their incredible lovemaking session. Like she was very familiar to him. It wouldn't have been out of the realm of possibility for Declan to forget someone he had slept with (he probably forgot more than he remembered if put to the test), but he knew that wasn't it. No way would he have forgotten sleeping with Marlee.

He'd talked to Joey briefly this morning before he met Marlee at the studio, letting him know about the fire. Joey and Kathy were flying out this morning and Declan wanted to thank his friend again for coming to his last game. He'd asked his family not to come. They'd come for his last regular season home game. And he'd wanted to totally concentrate on continuing on in the playoffs. So having a former teammate be there for him was a nice consolation prize.

At Joey's tentative probing about Declan and Marlee, Declan alluded to this feeling of knowing Marlee previously. It wasn't a past life thing—Declan didn't believe in that—more of a comfort he felt with Marlee. Joey had understood, had even mentioned he'd felt something similar the night he'd met Kathy.

Although Joey had married Kathy on the night they'd met, and Declan wasn't thinking beyond spending this week with Marlee.

But his feelings were kind of like that throw on Marlee's wooden rocking chair—it looked new, but was like the blanket that you'd wrap around yourself when you were a kid. Soft, familiar, comfortable. Not that it was easy with Marlee; she kept him on his toes both intellectually and most definitely physically, but it was comfortable.

Marlee's slender fingers traced the frames. "Most live here or nearby. I have two older sisters and one younger brother. The sisters are in the Boston area, both married with kids. The brother is in New York. He's single, no kids. My parents recently retired and they're in Florida for the winter, but they still have the house we grew up in—it's only a short drive from here."

"What did your parents retire from?"

"You mean besides the Boston winters?"

Declan smiled, glad that Marlee was being so light with him. Because of what he'd taken as her internal struggle to enter into a short-term fling with him, he thought she might be having buyer's remorse by now. Or worse, outright guilt. Declan had every intention of seeing Marlee all he could for the next week. Getting inside her warm body every chance he could. He didn't want to deal with having to coax her for an encore. He took from her tone that coaxing wouldn't be necessary.

"Yes, besides that."

"They were both professors at Boston College. Mom philosophy and dad chemistry."

"Apple doesn't fall far, and all that?"

"I guess. Academic life was all I knew, and it fits me well. How about you, Declan, what do your parents do? Brothers? Sisters?"

It was refreshing to meet someone that knew nothing about him. His background had been such an open book for so long. How many covers of *Sports Illustrated* had he graced over the years? Declan gave Marlee the condensed version of his youth.

Oldest child of three raised on a working farm in central Ohio. His dad had placed a football in Declan's hand at twenty months, and, the legend has it, he threw it nearly thirty yards. His father encouraged Declan's passion, but never pushed. His fondest memories were of playing catch with his father alongside the barn after the evening chores. They'd still done that whenever Declan went home. He had won two Super Bowl rings, but the only times he ever choked up was when he replayed the sweet memories of him and his dad.

"My father died two years ago. Car accident. That's when I started seriously thinking about retiring."

Marlee wound her arm around Declan's waist and gave him her warmth. "I'm so sorry, Declan. And your mother?"

Declan put his arms around Marlee and pulled her close, taking the comfort she offered. "Thanks. My mom's still on the farm. My youngest brother took it over—had intended to all along. He does a great job with it, too. He and his wife have three rugrats, and they're now enjoying the life I loved growing up."

He instinctively reached for his wallet to show Marlee the photos of his nieces and nephews, then realized he'd taken it from his jeans earlier to get a condom. And then later to get another one. The wallet was somewhere on the bedroom floor along with his socks, underwear, and every stitch that Marlee had been wearing.

"My sister and her husband live in Ohio too. Not far from the farm. They have two children. My niece made that scarf of mine you're wearing. Mom's in Grandma heaven, having them all so close to her."

"And you? Will you be adding to her nirvana?"

"Someday, sure. Definitely. I didn't want to think about it until now. Once I was off the road. I want to see my kids grow up, not just phone home to hear the latest.

"What about you, Marlee? Have you decided that your career and an occasional affair are enough to make you happy?"

THERE WAS NO JUDGMENT IN HIS VOICE, AND YET Marlee bristled at the "occasional affair" remark. Of course that was what Declan would think of her. Could she really blame him? She was climaxing against a door after knowing him a day. She supposed all the women in Declan's life could be lumped into the same pile. Was she any different? Yes.

Because she wasn't after Declan for anything more than tonight. And maybe tomorrow night. Oh, hell, for the whole week if she could manage it. Then Declan would be in New York and she'd get on with her life.

She backed away from his embrace and moved toward the arched entryway leading to the kitchen. "Funny you should ask. I've just recently decided that I indeed 'want to have it all,' whatever that means. Meeting Prince Charming, marriage, baby carriage, the whole nine yards." Marlee was surprised at her candor. She knew her intentions, but she hadn't shared them with anyone else.

After having been burned two years ago, she learned to keep her love life to herself. Or lack of love life.

First, she didn't want her friends' and family's pity if she never found a man she wanted to marry. She had thought about having a child without a husband. She wavered on that one, intending to put off that decision until she had thrown in the towel on the idea of a traditional marriage and family. Her clock was ticking, but at this point it was ticking softly.

Second, she didn't want those same friends and family making it their sole mission in life to find Marlee a husband. If it didn't happen for her, it didn't happen. She was very fulfilled in her career and could always bestow all her maternal yearnings upon her nieces and nephews. They already added so much to her life, brought her tremendous joy.

"So we're both at the point in our lives where we want to settle down and have a family? Hhhmm, maybe we should take a look at that, Marlee," he said with a light, almost teasing tone.

"Yeah. Right," she snorted. She entered the kitchen and turned on the light.

A STUNNED DECLAN FOLLOWED BEHIND.

Declan felt like he'd just been sacked by a three-hundred-pound defensive tackle. What was so funny about the idea? He'd said it lightly, so as to not scare Marlee off, but he hadn't intended for her to laugh. She had *snorted*, for Christ's sake. Did she think she could do that much better than him? They'd just proven they were compatible in the bedroom. Way compatible. Their upbringings were similar, their homes were nearly identical. Was she still deluding herself with the idea that they were total opposites?

Declan was about to make her see the light when he stopped himself. *What are you going to do then? Prove to her how much you have in common, how good you'd be together, how it could be more than just a week-long fling? That maybe they should seriously consider the possibility of a relationship? Then what? You get on a plane Sunday morning, and you have no idea what the next few weeks will hold, let alone the next few years.*

He hadn't lied when he'd told Marlee he was ready to settle down. But he needed to get his ducks in a row first. It would probably take one to two years before he truly had a handle on his future. He figured that if he did get on with a network, he would probably have to spend the first few years on the road, covering games. Eventually, he could work his way into a studio job, doing pre-game stuff. Maybe sitting next to Terry and Howie.

Could he ask Marlee to wait that long before entering into a permanent relationship? Would she, even if he asked her to? Her snort was probably all the answer he needed. Besides, Declan knew it wasn't fair, but he had no clock by which becoming a father was set. Marlee wanted kids, she couldn't realistically wait several years to begin a relationship with Declan, even though she was only thirty. Not that she'd even entertain the idea of something between them.

Boy, that snort had really gotten to him. But there was no sense dredging up what-ifs for something that couldn't happen.

"My God, I've died and gone to Cuisinart heaven," he murmured as he entered Marlee's kitchen. It was state of the art, and like her living room, was almost identical in style and layout to his. "This is great. I love it."

"Thank you. I love it too. It's my baby. It took me several years to get it just the way I want it. It's probably my favorite room in the house, the place I look most forward to when I get home."

The counters were a deep gray marble with flecks of green throughout. All the appliances were stainless steel and the cupboards all had glass doors. It was very organized, but every square inch of space on the counters was covered with gadgets. Bread maker, food processor, espresso machine. An island housed the oven and stovetop, and was done in the same marble.

Above it, steel pans hung from a scaffolding that was attached to the ceiling. Kitchen gadgets seemed to be Marlee's vice.

"Hey, you've got that new pasta maker. I've been meaning to pick that up. Have you used it? Do you love it? Is it better than the older model?"

"Yes. I do. And yes, it is better." Marlee was obviously startled to see Declan's enjoyment of her kitchen. He could see her puzzled look directed toward him, as if she was wondering if there was more to Declan Tate than just the body she'd just enjoyed.

He twirled around the room, taking another look. "I can cook for you this week after all. I'll just use your kitchen." He turned to look at her. "Or are you territorial?"

"Well, yes, usually. But you don't seem to be an amateur, so…I'll let you play in my sandbox."

Declan gave her a sly grin. "Yes indeedy, I do like playing in your box." He moved toward her, then, as if remembering what had brought them downstairs, veered toward her refrigerator. Quench that hunger first, then deal with the other one.

The hunger for Marlee.

He did sate himself, with both food and Marlee, well into the night.

Chapter 9

In the shower the next morning, Marlee noticed her body still bore the signs of Declan's loving. Reddened places on her body where his stubble had rubbed. Sensitive places internally where other parts of him had rubbed.

To be filled by Declan had been an experience like no other. Remembering that man, a warrior, a gladiator, a man who battled men three times his size, pounding into her with such a tender ferocity put Marlee on the brink of yet another orgasm as her hands slid over her body.

Regretfully, she pulled herself out of the bliss of remembering the previous night. She needed to get a move on if she wanted to be to the studio by ten.

She didn't have to be, she made her own schedule for this week, but she wanted to get right to work. She was excited about the additions she'd made yesterday with Declan's help. She wanted to quickly incorporate them into her speech and then practice the whole thing at least twice. Then it would be Declan's turn to practice.

The thought of getting that gorgeous man on camera

intoxicated her. She knew he had one of those faces that would photograph even better than he looked in person. And that was saying a lot; to top how good he looked up close and personal.

As she washed, Marlee's skin felt raw and sensitive. She felt no guilt from the previous evening's wantonness, only surprise. Surprise that she'd been so responsive to Declan's touch, to his kisses, to the words he used to take her higher. Surprise that she could give as good as she got, and Declan had seen that she'd definitely gotten. Surprise that being with Declan had seemed so natural to her, that they had quickly behaved as long-time lovers. And mostly, surprise at the yearning she felt to continue this affair.

Somewhere in the back of her mind, she'd harbored the thought that one night with Declan might cure her of this attraction. That they would mutually combust, taking with them this affinity they felt for each other's bodies. They'd combusted, all right. But instead of the flames burning themselves out, they only seemed to increase. At least for Marlee. She wouldn't assume that Declan felt what she did, though it sure seemed like he did. And he had made definite plans to see her again, only if it was for business reasons.

Declan had nudged her awake very early in the morning.

"I need to go to the hotel and change. I've got to meet the insurance people and the contractor at my house at eight. I don't know how long that will take, but I'll come to the studio right after. I'll bring us some lunch. I'm leaving my cell number on the dresser for you in case you need to get a hold of me before then. Do you have a way I can get a hold of you in the studio if my meetings run long?"

Marlee, barely audible, still nearly asleep, gave Declan her cell phone number, which he copied down and put in his jeans.

"Guess I'll have a phone number in my pants today, won't I. Man, do those women ever stop?"

Marlee moaned to show her acknowledgement of the joke and then showed Declan what she thought of his humor—by flipping him the bird. She flopped her arm back down; she hadn't even raised her head or looked at Declan.

"Marlee Reeves, Ph.D., flipping me off. Unbelievable." Declan chuckled, kissed the top of Marlee's head, told her to go back to sleep, and quietly left her bedroom.

BY ONE IN THE AFTERNOON, MARLEE FELT CONFIDENT that the suggestions Declan had made the day before would fit seamlessly into her lecture. She was also comfortable with the football terms, and that was key. Like Declan had said, people would spot a phony a mile off. He'd not only told her what would be appropriate, but explained exactly what each bit of jargon meant. That, coupled with the full-body demonstrations last night in bed, made her knowledge of the game almost passable. She made a final jot in her notes and then placed them in her bag. She was surprised Declan wasn't there yet. Her stomach rumbled, as if to agree with her.

Her cell phone rang and she rummaged through her satchel to find it. Probably Declan canceling, she thought. Then she wondered why she had instinctively thought he'd be canceling? He'd seemed eager to see her later when he'd left her bed this morning, had even joked with her. And even if he was canceling, where was this insecurity of hers coming from?

But she knew exactly where it came from.

"Hello."

"Marlee, it's Declan."

Just hearing his voice sent a tremble through her. She could close her eyes and hear that voice, low and gravelly, whispering in her ear, telling her when to come, as he'd done last night. She pulled herself away from her reverie and quickly tried to discern the tone of his voice. Business voice? A canceling voice? A last-night-was-great-but-you're-not-as-good-as-the-thousands-of-women-I've-been-with-so-sayanora voice? Did she get any of that from his simple three words? It didn't even occur to Marlee to temper her response to fit him, even if she could figure out his tone. She'd never learned to play the games that most women did, had thought they were asinine anyway.

"Hi, Declan."

"Listen, I'm stuck here at my house. This is taking a lot longer than I thought. There's more damage than anybody realized. I'm going to be here all afternoon, then I need to swing by the hotel and drop off the rest of my clothes for this week and the stuff I want to take to New York. I might as well take it all over there now, then I can leave the cleaning and repairs crew to it and not have to disturb them later in the week."

"I'm sorry it was worse than you thought. How disappointing."

"Yeah. So, lunch is obviously out. And it looks like I won't get to the studio before five, so me working with the camera is out today too."

Here it comes, she thought. *Next he'll tell you where he has to be tomorrow, so he can't make it then, and that he'll call.* Then that would be it—she'd never see him again.

Marlee's spirits fell. *Buck up*, she told herself. *You wanted one night with Declan and you got it. You were just being greedy hoping for more.* He wasn't the type to be with the same woman for any length of time. Apparently that length even applied to a week.

She steeled herself for what Declan would say next, how he

would get out of seeing her again. At least she'd gotten the stuff she needed for her lecture. She should be happy with that. That and one night of incredible sex with Declan.

"Here's what I'm thinking…Marlee, you still there?"

"Yes."

"Okay. I should be done around four. Why don't I go do some grocery shopping, meet you at your place when you're done, and cook you the best dinner you've ever had?"

The elation that ripped through Marlee scared her. She shouldn't be that excited that Declan wanted to see her again. But she was. So much so that the next thing out of her mouth came as a complete shock to her.

"Declan, why don't you stay with me this week, instead of a hotel?" She almost dropped her phone. Had she really just asked him to stay with her? Seconds ago she was waiting for a brush-off, and now she'd just invited Declan to be a guest in her home.

He'd probably received dozens of offers from the women who'd been at his house when he returned the night of the fire. He hadn't taken any of them up on it—what made her think he would accept her offer. And did she really want him to accept?

Yes. The idea of waking up beside Declan every morning this week thrilled her.

Declan's hesitation on the phone mirrored her doubts. She began mentally stammering, trying to figure out how to give Declan an out.

"Marlee…that would be great. That would help out a lot. I wasn't looking forward to spending this week in a hotel when I'm going to be in one all of next week too. I get pretty sick of hotels by the end of the season."

"Okay. So my house a little after five?"

"Deal. Are you sure you don't mind me staying with you? Because the hotel's fine, really."

"I don't mind. It makes sense. I'm only a few minutes from the studio, so you can easily get here when you want to work with the camera."

"Tomorrow. Definitely tomorrow. It'll be Wednesday already and I need all the practice I can get before I leave." His voice got low, and his drawl came back when he said, "There's something else I want to get all I can of before I leave."

"What?" But she knew what he would say. Hoped, anyway.

"You." He hung up, leaving Marlee tingling and aroused and anticipating going home more than she had in years.

Declan hung up the phone and continued his packing. The destination—if not the content—of the suitcases had changed. For the better, right? In retrospect, Declan wasn't sure. Marlee's offer of hospitality had so surprised him that he'd agreed before he could really weigh out the consequences.

But the consequences shouldn't be too serious. By making love last night and making her dinner tonight, Declan would already have invaded the two rooms Marlee probably most held dear. The two places that fed her body, anyway.

He'd received several offers of a place to stay this week, most from the women who were still at his house when he'd arrived Sunday night. But also some from his teammates. Declan didn't want to take any of them up on their offers. He thought he should be alone this week, or if not alone, at least not someone's guest. He'd hoped things would work out with Marlee, and he wanted to be able to come and go from her as he pleased.

This was now a double-edged sword. He was with Marlee,

but he couldn't very well come and go as he pleased, not when he was staying in her house and working with her during the days. Surprisingly, Declan didn't panic at the thought. In fact, he kind of liked it, which was why he'd said yes to Marlee's proposition so quickly.

Declan replayed their conversation in his mind. He wanted to be with her. In her home. Where she was comfortable.

Declan had seen Marlee's pure adoration when she'd shown him the pictures of her nieces and nephews last night. The way she'd traced her nephew's Styrofoam hook with a wistful smile on her face, as if she was right back in the moment, expecting to shield her eyes from the wayward appendage at any minute.

Declan had seen a softness in Marlee when she looked at those pictures. Not when they were in bed, though. There she had been passionate and responsive, but Declan didn't fool himself into believing that what Marlee felt for him was real. None of the women Declan was ever with had real sentiment for him. How could they? They never took the time to get to know him. The man he was away from the gridiron.

And just who was that man? Did he even know? He was going to have a hell of a lot of time to figure it out. All the time in the world. Just him, alone with his thoughts, becoming a man devoid of football.

Well, not totally devoid. Not if he got this network gig.

His stomach lurched at the thought, as it did every time he allowed himself to dwell on it. If he didn't get this, what would he do? He had enough money to last his entire lifetime. Had already set up trust funds for the educations of his nieces and nephews. Made sure the family farm would never be in need of anything, no matter how uncertain farming became. His mother was well taken care of. He'd bought her a condo in

Florida for if she ever got tired of Ohio winters on the farm. Realistically, he could just sit back and hobby his way to old age.

There was a flaw with that plan. Other than cooking, Declan didn't have many hobbies. He didn't even get to do much cooking during the season. He ate at the football offices most nights. A salad or eggs in the screening room while he watched video. In the off-season, he was a voracious reader, but even then, hobbies would take second place to his physical regimen. He would still work out several hours a day. More, as he got older and his body was more susceptible to injury.

The game of football had consumed his whole life, and he was grateful for all it had brought him. Incredible highs and lows, a pride in his body and accomplishments, riches, but most importantly to Declan, the feeling you got when you were on a team.

There was nothing like it. Being a part of making something happen. Knowing if you didn't do your best that the end result wasn't going to be pretty. Chewing guys out when they messed up. Praising them when they did well. Being a part of a team was precious to Declan.

Down deep, that was what he knew he'd miss most. Not the game itself, but the meshing of guys from all walks of life to achieve a common goal. Maybe he'd get lucky and have that kind of atmosphere with a broadcasting job. After all, most of those guys were retired players too, they probably craved that feeling as well. Declan didn't think you could achieve that level of camaraderie in a broadcasting booth, but he hoped it was possible. That thought alone kept him from falling into a deep despair over his retirement.

That was why working with Marlee in front of a camera was so important. He had given thousands of interviews during his career, both on camera and for the print media. But he had always either been on the field or in the locker room—in his element. Playing the role of sports hero. Most times he'd still been in his uniform, wearing it like a shield, only talking about the game and the team, never having to just be…Declan.

His agent had said they'd have professionals in New York to work with him, but he wanted to practice on his own first. He felt really comfortable with Marlee, assumed he still would even after they'd slept together, and he wanted her input. She obviously knew how to put a program together, and her ease in front of the camera yesterday was unmistakable.

She taught public speaking for a living, for Christ's sake.

Declan wasn't naive enough to believe that the networks would come calling on his reputation as one of the game's best quarterbacks alone. He needed to be able to hold his own on camera, and he also had to look good. Looks played a part in broadcasting, that was not to be denied. Why would ESPN put Kirk Herbstreit in blue shirts every week if not to capitalize on his baby blues?

Declan hadn't noticed until a woman had pointed it out to him, and, sure enough, the blond, blue-eyed former quarterback was seldom on air when he wasn't wearing a crisp dark blue shirt under his sports coat. Kirk was a former Ohio State quarterback too—maybe Declan should give him a call and get some inside scoop on this whole audition process.

He thought he could hold his own with the pretty boys of sports broadcasting. He wasn't vain, but knew he was considered a good-looking guy. The thought was hard to escape when he was approached several times throughout his career to do a beefcake calendar, or other endorsements. He always said no. Maybe he should have done a few of those things, so at least now it wouldn't all be so foreign to him.

Maybe if he had he'd feel as comfortable at all this as Marlee seemed to.

Declan didn't delude himself that it was all Marlee's delivery and content that made her such a riveting speaker. Just to watch her was a pleasure. Her poise, her confidence that showed through when she spoke were obvious. Classy. Declan thought the word was overused, but it definitely fit Marlee. Maybe he was so drawn to her because there was a definite lack of classy women in Declan's circle. Whatever. He thought she was classy, and a great speaker, and he was spending the week at her house, the nights in her bed.

Heaven.

He went downstairs after packing two bags. One for this week with Marlee, filled with jeans and shirts. The other for next week. A garment bag with a few suits. His agent said that they'd have what they wanted him to wear for the taping in New York already, so Declan only needed to bring some suits to wear to meetings with the networks. Years of traveling had taught Declan to pack light.

He checked in one last time with the repair guys in the kitchen, making sure they had everything they needed. He surveyed his damaged kitchen one more time and knew he needed to get out of there before he broke down and bawled like a baby over the disorder of his pride and joy.

Disappointing. That was the word Marlee had used when he told her about the fire damage. Even that set Marlee apart from the other women in his life. Bummer. Drag. Those are words they would have used. But "disappointing" seemed to fit the situation to a tee. It was disappointing. The kitchen he loved was not entirely destroyed, but would have to have major renovations done. Declan had taken the opportunity to make some changes in the kitchen. He'd designed it with the contractor six years ago when he'd had the house built, but years of usage had given him some suggestions on how to have it improved.

He hadn't had much food in the fridge. The party had been catered and the leftovers were taken to a homeless shelter, per Declan's request. He purposely didn't want much food in the house because of him leaving for a week on Sunday. Declan didn't get a chance to cook much during the season, anyway.

He cleaned out the refrigerator and freezer because the power would be off in the kitchen for the next several days when the crews began the repairs. He took the few things that would travel well and put them in a box to take to Marlee's. The rest he put in a bag to take to the same shelter that he'd told the caterers about.

The NFL was very active with United Way, and Declan had been involved with them and several other charitable organizations his entire career. Before that, really. His parents had instilled in Declan a sense of community, a basic goodness toward his fellow man. Declan had always had the "there but for the grace of God go I" mentality, knowing full well he'd been blessed with a talent that few men possessed. He acknowledged it as well as stood in awe of it.

Declan could have easily had his cleaning lady take care of all this, but figured this would save her from having to come in at all. She came in twice a week and stocked the fridge, did the laundry and cleaning. Declan had called her and told her to come in only on Friday to see if the crews needed anything and to dispose of any of their trash. He then gave her next week off completely, asking her to come back the following Monday with groceries, as Declan was due to arrive back from New York that Monday night.

With the home front taken care of, Declan left with all he would need for the next two weeks.

After stopping by the shelter, taking the time to meet some of the people in attendance and signing a few autographs for them, he spent a couple of hours in the grocery store. He had found a gourmet store in Newton a few years ago. Not too far from where Marlee lived, he now realized. He traveled the aisles several times, feeling produce, sniffing fresh herbs, debating the choices. Marlee being a vegetarian like himself worked out great. Should he impress her with something sleek and ultra nouveau, or go with basic Midwest home-style cooking? He could do both well.

The thought of how badly he wanted to impress Marlee only slightly irritated him. He was starting to get used to the idea of needing Marlee to see he wasn't just a womanizing, one-night-stand kind of guy. Surely she didn't still think about him in those terms? Not after the day they had spent together yesterday. Or the night.

That, coupled with the fact that he'd accepted her invitation to stay with her this week, should at least let Marlee know she was more than a one-night stand to him. She was more than a week-long stand to him, but he didn't think she'd want to hear that from him. Not yet, anyway. He had time to work on her.

He was still working on those thoughts himself.

He had a fleeting vision of her wooden frames and his silver ones intermingled on a larger mantel, with maybe some golden ones with their own kids photos interspersed between them.

Where had that thought come from? Still, the vision was crystal clear, and Declan hung on to it for a second or two before he let it drop, like his receivers sometimes did when Declan's passes were too strong and fierce to hang on to.

He ended up buying the ingredients for both types of meals, thinking that now that he was staying with Marlee, he'd get the chance to show off all his skills. And not just his skills in the kitchen. He smiled to himself.

As he neared her home, Declan was once again struck with the feel of familiarity and comfort he found when driving through Marlee's neighborhood. The trees were bare of leaves, of course, but Declan could picture the powerful oaks and elms that lined the streets at their brilliant fall hues of oranges and reds.

There were kids playing street hockey on her road, and they stopped, moving their nets out of the way as Declan's vehicle came into view. Declan was surprised to feel a lump in his throat as he watched the kids. He and his siblings had played such games. He hoped his children someday would too. The vision of teaching a son to catch a football flashed before him, and he felt the image warm him, flow through his body like a shot of alcohol. He let his daydream continue and was not surprised to see Marlee coming out of a back door and call them in to dinner.

Simple stuff, but it felt right to Declan.

Marlee's garage was open and her car was parked far to one side of the attached two-car garage. Leaving a space for him? She would have closed the door otherwise, right? In Boston winters, you definitely wanted to put your car in the garage overnight. It saved you lots of time in the morning. Declan had spent almost twenty minutes this morning scraping the ice and snow from his windshield, waiting for his car in Marlee's driveway to warm up.

He parked his car in the garage and headed to the inside door that led to the kitchen. He took a couple of bags of groceries. He'd come back for the rest and his suitcases. He pressed the garage door button next to the door leading to the kitchen and watched as the door lowered, closing out the twilight and the blustery wind.

Marlee was standing at the island in the middle of the kitchen. She had what looked like a glass of water in her hand and she was leaning over, reading a newspaper that was spread out across the marble countertop. She was wearing a maroon Boston College sweatshirt and black yoga pants, her hair pulled into a ponytail, and Declan thought she looked about twenty years old. She glanced up at him as he entered and pushed her glasses up her nose. Declan had seen her do that a couple of times yesterday as she went through her speech and found the habit endearing—sexy, even.

She smiled. A warm, intimate smile, and in that moment Declan knew he'd made a good decision about staying with Marlee. It felt…right. Coming home to this woman with a car full of groceries on a cold winter's night. Perfect.

He returned her smile and greeted her with, "Hi, honey. I'm home!"

A soft sort of giggle came out of Marlee. "It's about time. I'm starving!"

Declan's grin drew wider. He knew what would fill Marlee up.

And then afterward, he'd feed her.

Chapter 10

Marlee was not to be swayed. Not even for hot sex with Declan. She wanted to see his stuff, all right, but his cooking skills were the prowess she wanted demonstrated first. Hearing the garage door go down behind him, seeing him walk into her kitchen laden with groceries, even now as he put them away, getting the lay of the land of her cupboards, it all felt so natural, like something they'd done for years.

Marlee scolded herself. It wasn't about Declan. It just demonstrated to her how ready she was to be a unit, to share her life and her home—and yes, even her kitchen—with a man. Now that she was certain this was the future she wanted, she could start the search for a viable candidate. And the short list didn't include Declan Tate.

From somewhere deep inside of her—and Marlee was pretty sure that spot was at the place between her thighs—a voice screamed, *Why not Declan?* It was not the first time the analytical side of her debated the emotional side, but it was the closest match they'd had in years.

Marlee would let the emotional side rarely win, and the

events usually included standing in front of rack of designer suits that weren't on sale. She wasn't about to be waylaid by her attraction to Declan—and that was all it was, she kept reminding herself—on an issue so important.

Doing just that had almost destroyed her two years ago.

She'd met Justin Jones in an aisle at the gourmet grocery store in Newton. He'd asked her what was the difference between arugula and kale, and his gorgeous blue eyes had her saying yes to his offer of coffee.

It had been a whirlwind romance, and before she knew it, she was deeply in love with Justin. At first, the thought that he was the star shortstop for the Boston Red Sox was kind of cool. She'd never followed sports so hadn't known who he was until their third date, but it was summertime and she'd gone to the games, sitting with the players's wives and girlfriends (WAGs, she later found out). She'd been amused at the attention she'd garnered as Justin's girlfriend.

He was on the road a lot, sometimes for ten days or longer, but when the Sox were in town, they spent as much time as possible together. Within four months, Marlee was nearly living at Justin's amazing Boston penthouse apartment and they were talking—albeit abstractedly—about a permanent future together.

His place was beautiful, with a breathtaking view, but it was decorated in a very modern—almost cold—way, and Marlee never felt quite at home. Though she loved being there with Justin.

He told her how much he loved her, and Marlee had felt the same way. Their lovemaking had been both lusty and sweet, and Marlee savored lying in Justin's arms throughout the night.

Until someone with an anonymous Gmail account had sent her a link to a sports gossip site that featured the Top Ten

Players of Baseball. And it had nothing to do with their prowess on the field.

Justin was number three.

At first, Marlee assumed that the list was from the pre-Marlee Justin's antics. But there were pictures on the site of Justin with women where he was wearing a shirt Marlee had bought him.

She'd confronted him, of course. And he didn't deny any of it. In fact, he seemed somewhat shocked that Marlee didn't know "the score," as he called it. "That's my world, babe. It's just understood that…things happen…when I'm on the road. But I come home to you, Marlee. And when I'm in Boston, you're the only…" He'd stopped then at the horrified look on her face. She'd turned from him and went to the bedroom to pack her things, leaving his apartment, and Justin, that night.

She'd been devastated. And what was worse than having her heart broken was her stupid pride. Not only had he cheated on her, he hadn't even tried very hard to cover it up. And certainly didn't deny it when she'd confronted him.

Her family and friends had rallied behind her. She'd even flown to Portland for a long weekend with Kathy to try and ease the pain and humiliation. They'd gone shopping, and drinking, and had a great time. One of Kathy's sisters was getting married soon and they'd gone shopping for shoes for Kathy to wear with her bridesmaid dress. Over margaritas they'd both gotten a little weepy over their lack of someone special. Then they'd made a makeshift voodoo doll of Justin Jones and rubbed it in the salt on the rim of their drinks.

It was just what she needed, but then Marlee came home just in time to see Justin's face plastered all over the Boston papers during the World Series, and she felt the wounds opening all over again.

It had taken time, as all broken hearts did. And Marlee

was *just* to the point where she was willing to brave the dating world to find the man she could settle down with and start the family she badly wanted.

But she wasn't stupid enough to think that it would ever be another pro athlete who traveled all the time.

"MARLEE? MARLEE? WHERE DID YOU GO?"

Declan turned from putting away the groceries to see Marlee, water glass frozen halfway to her mouth, deep in thought.

"Nowhere, Declan. We're going nowhere," she said. Her shoulders drooped every so slightly and her head bowed. He knew those body movements, had copied them his fair share over his career.

It was the motion of defeat.

Dinner was good, one of his best. Marlee said she wasn't sure she could do better herself. Declan laughed. He liked that she didn't fawn over him, but geez, she could do a little better than that after the awesome meal he'd just fed her. "That's the most back-handed compliment I've ever received, and believe me, I've gotten a lot of those."

"Actually, if you knew how well I cooked, it wouldn't seem back-handed at all."

"That sounds like a challenge, Professor Reeves. All right, it's your turn tomorrow night."

"Deal." They shook on it and began clearing the table. They settled into an easy routine of doing the dishes. Marlee had a dishwasher, but they both lined up at the sink, seeking the physical contact they got by Declan washing and Marlee drying.

He was happy that she was joking with him. After that cryptic "We're going nowhere" comment earlier, she'd been very quiet. She'd watched intently while he'd prepared a spectacular fresh pesto sauce and made spinach pasta, but only spoke when he didn't know where to find something in the unfamiliar kitchen.

Hip to hip, they finished the last of the dishes. Drying their hands on a dishtowel at the same time, they tangled both the towel and their fingers, drying each other, looking for any excuse to touch.

"What's on the menu for dessert, Chef Tate?"

Declan handed the towel to Marlee and walked to the refrigerator to retrieve the item he had placed there earlier. He turned and held it up to Marlee.

"A can of Reddi-wip? What's it go on?"

He gave her a grin as he walked by, taking her hand as he passed, and led her from the immaculate kitchen to the stairs. "You'll see," was all the answer he gave.

And she did.

Later, Declan put his stuff away in Marlee's closet. She'd also cleared out a drawer for him in her dresser. Neither one spoke about how smooth this transition seemed to be. Declan, having been an athlete his whole life, was very superstitious and reasoned that talking about how natural this all felt could possibly jinx it. He put the book he was currently reading on the left-hand bedside table, just as he'd envisioned the first time he saw Marlee's bedroom. But they didn't get any reading done during the night, though they were certainly up late. They didn't get much sleep, either.

They continued in their domesticity the following morning. Declan made a feta omelet, which they shared, and Marlee packed them both a lunch of the leftover pasta to take to the studio.

He came up behind her while she stood in front of her closet, contemplating which suit to wear. When Declan saw a few pairs of jeans in the closet, he tried talking her into discarding her suits in favor of denim.

"But I always wear suits when I'm working. Just because you can spend your workday in T-shirts and jock straps doesn't mean I can."

The vision of Marlee in a skin-tight T-shirt and the female equivalent of a jockstrap—a thong—raced through Declan's mind. It'd be a short tee, too, showing lots of Marlee's smooth, white tummy, and hugging her amazing breasts.

"Do you have to be anywhere but the studio today?"

"No."

"Then come on, wear something casual. I'm wearing jeans."

She hesitated. Declan realized that her wardrobe was a type of armor for Marlee. It projected the image she strove to achieve: conservative, stylish, polished, professional. But did she really need to uphold that image with Declan? The man had seen her in much, much less over the last two nights. And she wouldn't be taping herself at all today, just Declan, so ultimately she let him talk her into heeding his request.

Over her cream satin panties and bra, which Declan had personally picked out for her, she donned jeans and a soft cashmere turtleneck sweater in a green that complemented her eyes and auburn hair. She even wore her hair down, and Declan figured this was indeed a triumph. She still wore the tortoiseshell glasses, but Declan had come to like them and didn't want to suggest she lose the specs as well. They were part of the Marlee he envisioned.

At first Declan was going to object to the high-necked sweater until he saw how clingy the garment was. It cradled her curves and left very little to Declan's imagination. Not that he didn't have the sight of Marlee's naked body seared into his mind. He'd studied her body so closely last night during their lovemaking that he'd never have to imagine anything about Marlee ever again. The memories would always be crystal clear.

The drive to campus was short and filled with merriment as he regaled Marlee with a story of his brother and he trying to milk their first cow on the farm when they were kids. He had Marlee near tears of laughter, and she placed her hand on his arm as he drove. A current of electricity and heat shot through the many layers of winter clothing they were both wearing, as it always seemed to whenever they touched. Their eyes met for a moment, then they both looked away, lost in their own thoughts, smiles on their faces.

IN THE AFTERNOON, THEY SAT IN THE TALK-SHOW CHAIRS and ate the leftover pasta, which Marlee warmed up in the microwave. They were both happy with the work they'd done in the morning.

They'd set up the camera facing the newscaster stage and filmed Declan behind the desk on one side. Marlee had checked scores from NBA, NHL, and college basketball games from her home office earlier while Declan was making their breakfast, and placed printouts on the desk for Declan to read.

He'd been as delectable on camera as Marlee had imagined he'd be. The green of his eyes was mesmerizing, and the rich sheen off his wavy hair made it seem even more luxurious. And she knew firsthand how soft it was. His broad shoulders and sturdy chest seemed to shoot from behind the desk like a sturdy tree trunk rising from the ground. He had that deadly combination of being drop-dead gorgeous and instilling confidence and trustworthiness at the same time.

He was a natural. The scores rolled off his tongue and Declan even winged it a few times, adding fake stats and pronouncing several Russian-born hockey players' names with ease. At least, Marlee thought Declan got them right. Athletes' names were all Greek, or in this case Russian, to her.

As she ate her lunch, once again appreciating Declan's culinary skills, Marlee thought back to the session.

"You were really good. You have nothing to worry about. You're going to be great next week. The networks will be fighting over you." She had tossed her boots off and was now sitting in the big chair with her stockinged feet curled under her legs.

"Thanks. Yeah, it was okay. It should be all right next week. Guess I was worried over nothing."

"Well, I wouldn't exactly call your future nothing."

He shifted in his chair uncomfortably, almost dropping the paper plate that was resting on his lap. Marlee picked up on it immediately. This man was never anything but completely at home in his remarkable body. She quickly replayed the taping in her head to come up with an explanation.

"Declan?"

"Hmmm?" He shoveled another forkful to his mouth. The man did have an appetite. Which was fine with her—anything to keep his furnace stoked.

"Did you enjoy it? The being on camera, I mean?"

"It wasn't as uncomfortable as I thought it'd be."

"But did you *enjoy* it? Do you think you'll enjoy broadcasting?"

He rose and took his now empty plate and plastic utensils to the garbage can. He looked to Marlee's lap to see if she was done, and when she indicated she was, he discarded hers as well. Then he sat back down in the chair and stretched out his long legs in front of him. They almost touched Marlee's chair, and if she'd had her feet on the ground they would have made contact.

She sensed he was stalling, but she didn't repeat the question or change the topic. She waited.

"Enjoy? No." As she made to comment on that, he rushed on, "But I'm not really sure what I'll enjoy anymore. I did something I loved for my entire life, a living little boys grow up dreaming of, and I never, not for one day, took it for granted. I know how fortunate I've been. I can't expect the rest of my career, whatever that entails, to be nearly as rewarding."

"I guess not. Still, that sounds so, I don't know, final. I don't have any pity for you, Declan—you're right, most people would love the life you've had, but…" She was not sure what she wanted to say, or if Declan even wanted to hear it.

"But what?"

"Well, just because you're grateful for your past doesn't mean you can't desire a future that will be as fulfilling. You might not get it, but you certainly won't if you don't think you deserve it."

He mulled on that for a second, slowly nodding. "Yeah, I get that. You're probably right."

"So, if you decide you're allowed to love the next phase of your life as much as the previous one, what steps do you take to ensure you get it?"

"Pretty heady stuff. Sure you aren't a shrink and not a professor?"

"No. You'll get no analysis from me. It's just…I've asked myself a lot of those same questions recently."

"Yeah? And how are *you* going to get over being a sports hero?"

"Okay, we're coming from slightly different places…"

"Not really. I was only teasing. From what you said before,

we're at the same place, trying to figure out how to get to the next phase."

"Exactly. It just so happens our next phases are completely different."

He shrugged his broad shoulders. "I wouldn't even say that. Your next phase includes getting married and starting a family, right?"

At Marlee's nod, Declan continued, "Mine too, eventually. I just need to get a handle on what I'll be doing for a living first. But marriage and kids is definitely in the plan." He said the last part slowly, and met her eyes as he delivered the information.

She felt a moment of panic, which quickly subsided. Surely he didn't mean her as a candidate. He knew as well as she did that their lives were too different to be anything more than a week-long fling. And there was no way in hell she'd ever let herself become involved long-term with a pro athlete again. She didn't think she could go through that kind of pain again.

Even if the sex with Declan was the best she'd ever had.

"For a smart woman, you sure can be stupid," he mumbled under his breath, but Marlee heard.

"What the hell is that supposed to mean?"

"It means you've put a label on me—if only in your mind — and reduced my future, and that of my family-to-be, to some level that you would never stoop to."

He was angry now, and Marlee had never seen him angry. Even the night they'd met, after a brutal loss and the end of his career, he'd been nothing but jovial. Kathy had made some comment about the famous Tate temper on the field, and Marlee was now seeing it up close.

"Declan, you obviously think you saw some reaction from me that just wasn't there," she said, not quite truthfully.

"It was there, Marlee, and you know it." He leaned

forward in the chair, his legs coming up as he rested his forearms on his knees. A flush of red rushed his face.

"Okay, then. What was it you think you saw from me?"

"Panic."

"Panic? Declan, I don't panic."

"It was panic, all right. You saw where I was going, and the thought repulsed you. You were trying to figure out how to stop the line of conversation. Fast."

Damn, how could he know her so well? Decipher her looks so easily? Still, she didn't want to hurt him, so she'd bluff her way through. "I have no idea what you're talking about. I think we should get back to work." Cutting off a possible response, she rose and went to the laptop.

Declan didn't say another word.

Chapter 11

Marlee *had* known where Declan was going. Or at least she thought she did. His future wife and children. She didn't want to think about them, this mythical woman she began conjuring up when he mentioned a family. Instantly a picture formed of a woman wearing spandex and three-inch heels, and cracking gum while she balanced a son that looked just like Declan on her hip. The image was meant to amuse Marlee, to lessen the hurt she felt that it wouldn't be her hip Declan's son dangled from, but it didn't. She was surprised at how much her heart ached, and that emotion was what threw the look of panic into her eyes.

She could talk with Declan about his future profession, even about a far-off family, in generalities, but she didn't want to hear any specifics. She didn't want to put a face and, heaven forbid, a name to the woman who would get to share Declan's life. She didn't know if Declan had already chosen a candidate from the myriad of women in his life to be the mother of his children, and she didn't want to.

They were lovers, and with time spent together in the

studio and Marlee's kitchen, they were also becoming friends. She had encouraged Declan to confide in her about his misgivings attached to the broadcasting career he was pursuing. She couldn't in all fairness decree that he couldn't discuss anything more personal. That must have been why Declan got so upset.

She hadn't been fair to him. But who ever said life was fair?

Still, a niggling of a notion crept into Marlee's brain. What if there wasn't a particular woman in Declan's agenda? What if the deliberate eye contact and slowing of speech for emphasis when speaking his plan *was* to get Marlee's attention? So that Marlee would sit up and take notice that she and Declan wanted the same things out of life. Could he possibly have her in mind when he spoke of the future?

That thought brought a whole different type of panic to Marlee, and she almost stumbled over the TV cart as she was loading the file they'd made of Declan.

The rest of the afternoon was spent working. They watched the tape of Declan's performance from the morning. Marlee gave a few suggestions—simple stuff, like for Declan to watch the use of hands. He tended to wave them around and make gestures while he talked. He nodded, and she could see he was absorbing all she said. She even gave him some simple tips she'd given different politicians over the year about holding a pen so that his hand felt more weighted and less likely to wave about.

They edited the file in iMovie, taking out the spots where they'd stopped and discussed things, then copied it to a thumb drive that they put in Marlee's satchel for Declan to take with him to New York. He'd take all the files they'd film in the next two days to give the professionals in New York an idea of Declan's weak spots, and bring them up to speed with his ability.

"Thanks, Marlee. Good tips. Let me think about them, then I'd like to try it again tomorrow. Is that okay with you?"

"Absolutely. Let's do you again tomorrow and then on Friday, if you're still willing, I'd like to try some of the basketball things you were talking about for my lecture."

"I'm more than willing, I'd love to tailor your stuff for each university. I love college sports, all kinds, and I still follow them all really closely. My Buckeyes aren't doing so well in B-ball this winter, but the Big Ten could have a shot at a couple of spots in the Final Four this March."

Marlee grasped maybe half of that analysis, but didn't press for clarification. It really wouldn't matter after this week, anyway. "Thanks. If we're done here, let's go home. It's my night to cook for you."

It became a ritual for them. That is, if you could create a ritual after three nights. A sumptuous dinner that tickled their taste buds. Warm conversation filled with childhood anecdotes from both their families. Then the hours of being together without intimately touching each other would become too much, and their desire would win out.

After hours of making love, Declan would invariably slip on his jeans, throw his shirt at her, and make for the kitchen. She always added his scarf to the ensemble, stopping to retrieve it from wherever he'd discarded it.

He would glide through the living room like it was his own, and he'd remark, once again, at how much alike their homes were.

"Same living room layout, same photos above the mantel, same appliances, I'm going to start feeling spooked if there's a pint of Häagen-Dazs Dulce de Leche in the freezer," he said as he entered the kitchen.

Marlee stopped in her tracks as Declan mentioned her midnight vice. "There isn't *a* pint. There are several." She was starting to feel spooked too. Much to her chagrin, she hadn't seen Declan's kitchen the night of the party, and his living room had been swamped with people so she didn't get a good look at it. But if he were telling the truth about how similar their houses were, coupled with this new discovery about the ice cream…she didn't want to think about it.

They looked at each other, their gazes meeting. Declan's look seemed confident, as if he had just confirmed something to himself. Marlee's was a little stunned, finding it hard to believe that she and a football player could really have the same style, goals, and interests, right down to the same taste in ice cream.

"God, I love this stuff. I like to put mine in the microwave for a few seconds to soften it up." He raised his eyebrows at her, as if to get her consent, and she did a "be my guest" gesture toward the microwave.

"You'll find that fifteen seconds on my microwave makes it just soft enough for the spoon to go easily through, but not soupy."

He grinned at her over his shoulder. "God, what a woman. I can't believe no man has snatched you up yet. Oh, that's right, you don't like sports…that must be it." He put the ice cream in and tuned in fifteen seconds on the microwave, then turned to her. He leaned up against the counter, his hands resting along the marble counter top at his hips, and watched her with a teasing smile on his face.

She moved to his side to get a spoon from a drawer and gave him a good-natured jab to his ribs with her elbow. When he groaned louder than necessary and feigned pain, she teased him back. "I thought football players were supposed to be tough. Can't take a nudge from a little ol' girl?"

He pivoted and stood behind her, his hips pinning her to the counter. He reached around and fondled her breasts through her shirt. *His shirt*, she reminded herself. He'd said liked seeing her in his shirt, and she loved wearing it, smelling Declan on herself.

Her breasts were full and heavy and he lifted them as he squeezed. "Darlin', there ain't nothing little about you. Especially these." He tweaked her nipples as the bell from the microwave dinged, and for just an instant Marlee thought her sensitized breasts had signaled their readiness.

He bent his head to her neck and nuzzled aside his scarf then licked her skin. They had both worked up a healthy sweat during sex, and she knew she probably tasted of salt and sweat. Of passion. The thought of tasting Declan in turn made her forget about the ice cream.

He ground the beginnings of an erection into her ass.

"Nah unh. No way, mister, keep that thing away from me. Not until I get some sustenance." Marlee could reach the microwave from where Declan had her pinned in. The container was still very cold to the touch, but the consistency was just as she had described. She sliced her spoon through the confection and reached it over her shoulder for Declan. "I will be nice and let you have the first bite."

"I intend to have the first and last bite, Marlee, and not necessarily of ice cream." He cleaned the spoon of ice cream and moved back to his original spot against the counter. Marlee turned around and leaned her behind against it as well, so they stood side by side. All the better to share.

Marlee held the pint while Declan took turns spoon-feeding her and then himself. It was no accident that his arm brushed across her breasts each time he reached for more. Their moans of ecstasy as they consumed the ice cream echoed the moans they had made upstairs a short time ago.

"Okay, switch. Give me the spoon. Holding this thing is freezing my hand." Marlee reached for the spoon handle and pushed the pint at Declan. He took the ice cream and grudgingly gave her the utensil.

"Crybaby."

"Oh yeah? Feel how cold." Marlee lifted her frigid fingers, intending on placing them on Declan's cheek. At the last moment, her hand detoured and she placed them instead on Declan's bared nipple. He instantly stiffened and let out a groan.

"Oh God. I don't know if that feels incredible or horrible. But Christ, don't stop."

Marlee had no intention of stopping after she saw how it affected him. She pivoted to stand in front of him. Face to face. Due to Declan's height it was more like face to chin, but Marlee had her sights set lower anyway.

She continued to stroke his nipple with her cold fingers as she kissed his neck. She quickly moved her way down his neck and collarbone, planting light kisses along the way. He smelled of musk and man, and it was heaven. How can anyone who looked so good smell that much better? She took a small step back to gaze at this astonishing specimen of physical supremacy. His chest was incredible. Broad, strong, leading to exceptional shoulders.

She had wondered in the restaurant the night they'd met if his shoulders could possibly look as good naked as they had underneath his crisp white shirt. They did. His chest was heavily sprinkled with hair that was both soft and coarse, and she reveled in the texture of it. The hair covered the great expanse of his chest, and then tapered off into a fine line down his six-pack abs and beyond, to the fly of his jeans. *All in good time, Marlee. You'll get there, but enjoy the trip down.*

She scooped another spoonful of ice cream and fed it to Declan as her mouth latched on to his other nipple.

"Mmmm, good. Ice cream that is," Declan said.

"Darlin'," Marlee said, mimicking Declan's drawl, "in about ten minutes you're not even going to be able to figure out which end of that spoon goes in your mouth." She gave a playful bite to his nipple as her hands moved down his sides, over his impossibly hard stomach, to rest at the top of his jeans. The metal of the cold spoon she held brushed across his side and he shuddered.

"Big talk."

"Oh, I can talk big, all right. What words do you want to hear come out of my mouth, Declan?" Marlee had never been verbally bold with a lover. She had responded to Declan's whispered intimacies, but she'd never instigated them. She had assumed that talking dirty during lovemaking just wasn't something she was comfortable with. Now she realized she hadn't done it because she had never had a partner whom she trusted so much.

During their earlier session, Declan had whispered all the things he was doing to Marlee and how it made him feel. What did they call that in the sports world? Play by play? If the way Marlee had responded to it was any indication, Declan would go far in broadcasting. He certainly was there already as a lover.

She didn't allow her mind to contemplate how many women on whom Declan had perfected this craft. For once, the off switch in her mind worked and she gave herself up to the perfect sensations that being with Declan gave her.

"Tell me you want me, Marlee."

"I want you, Declan." To prove her point, Marlee reached her hand into Declan's jeans and clasped his erect penis. Steel.

And it was all hers for the rest of the week. She could almost feel Declan's heart beating by just holding his penis. It was obvious to Marlee that the desperate wanting went both ways. It gave her the fortitude to go on.

"What else do you want to hear from me?" she asked.

Declan tilted her chin to meet his gaze. "Tell me how my cock feels, Marlee."

Marlee felt her moistness begin. Just hearing Declan say things like that to her made her wet. She was shocked at how easily he could arouse passion within her. She wasn't wearing any panties beneath his shirt, and she felt slick at the tops of her thighs.

"Your cock feels happy to see me." As Marlee said the word "cock" out loud, he hardened even more and she gently squeezed his shaft. Feeling him jerk in return put a small grin on her well-used lips. Lips that were swollen and red from his kisses.

"Oh, it is that. Definitely."

Marlee fed another spoonful of ice cream to first Declan and then herself. The spoon was in her right hand, her left hand firmly grasping him, her thumb brushing over his tip.

"What else? What else do you want to hear?"

"Tell me what you're going to do to my cock, Marlee."

"I can't, Declan."

"Why not?"

"Because I'm about to have my mouth full."

She took the pint of ice cream from Declan's hand, and, with the spoon, went down to her knees. She placed the ice cream on the floor beside Declan's foot, well within her reach. She stuck the spoon in the ice cream to allow both hands freedom.

She put her hands just inside the waistband of Declan's

jeans, then slid them down, bringing his jeans with them, careful to ease his full erection out of the well-worn material. His freed penis rose from his hair as if at attention. She pushed the jeans down to Declan's ankles, but when he made to step out of them, she stilled his legs.

She wanted him just like that. At her mercy, as she'd been their first night together, when he had given her such an intense orgasm up against the door. She ran her hands up his heavily muscled thighs. In the back of her mind ran the thought that she'd never have a lover that was so toned, so rock hard, so, so…Declan.

She reached down and scooped up a spoonful of the ice cream. She smeared small amounts on his testicles.

"God, Marlee." He hissed. He reached for her head, but she brushed him aside.

"Hands on the counter, Mr. Quarterback. I'm calling the plays now."

Declan placed his hands on the counter, his fingers curling around the marble edge. His sac was heavy and tightening as Marlee licked it clean of the rich ice cream. She took the spoon and dabbed more of the sweet substance there, and also at the tip of his penis, where a drop of his milky fluid had formed. The white cream of Declan blended in smoothly with the Häagen-Dazs. She lowered her head once again to lick Declan clean. Her tongue darted out like a kitten at a bowl of milk.

She could feel his eyes on the top of her head. She looked up as she moved her lips from his balls to the head of his shaft, meeting his deep green eyes. As she took him into her mouth, she watched as his pupils totally dilated, turning his eyes almost jade.

God, he was gorgeous. And for now, he was hers. The

thought jarred Marlee. She'd never been possessive before, not even with Justin. But then, she had never had her mouth around Declan Tate's hard cock before, either.

That changed everything.

Her tongue whirled around the engorged purple head, taking the ice cream off in one swoop, but she kept going. The rough texture of her tongue played along his ridge and she tapped it against the underside and felt his shudder.

Oh, Declan, you are so close. I love that I can do this to you. How many women have you had in your lifetime, and me, Marlee Reeves, can make you respond so intensely.

The confidence that thought gave her bolstered her onward. She leaned back onto her haunches and again made eye contact with Declan. He made to move, but, at her raised brow, kept his hands on the counter. He watched as she reached for the pint of ice cream. She took a medium-sized spoonful and held the utensil in an extended reach for Declan. He leaned down and took the bite. She then took a larger spoonful and set the container back on the floor.

As Declan watched her, she put the entire spoonful in her mouth. She then put the empty spoon back into the now nearly empty pint. She sat with the mouthful of ice cream. She didn't touch him in any way, but kept her eyes locked with his. She saw the question in his eyes, and she gave a slight nod of reassurance, as if to say, "Relax, I know what I'm doing." Even though she had no idea what she was doing.

As the seconds went by, her cheeks deflated as the ice cream melted in her mouth. She could almost see him thinking, *Her mouth must be ice cold.* Then she saw the moment in his eyes when he got it. He realized her intent just as Marlee swallowed the remaining ice cream, placed her hands on his thighs, leaned forward, and took Declan fully into her mouth.

He gasped. "Marlee, good God, that feels…incredible." The cold, sticky cavern of her mouth as she took in all of him sent a shudder through his gorgeous body.

He reached for Marlee's head, and came into contact with his scarf that was still around her neck and draped across her breasts. He grabbed the scarf on both sides of her and pulled up. It slid to the back of her neck and lodged at her nape. He pulled again, bringing her entire head even closer to his body.

Marlee had turned her mouth into a tingling, cool, sensation-driven vacuum. She sucked hard on Declan's shaft and brought her hands back to his balls to squeeze and caress. Her tongue, so cold, began to thaw from the intense heat of Declan's erection. She continued to swirl as she moved her head up and down his shaft.

He wound the excess material of the scarf around his hands. "Marlee. Darlin'. I'm gonna come." He tried to lift Marlee's head by tugging on the scarf, but she was having none of it. She clasped one hand around his iron-hard thigh and wrapped the other hand around the base of his shaft, stroking him quickly as her sucking motion increased, quickened.

Declan tried to protest again, but the jerking spasms of his body took over instead. He groaned, and swore, and bucked into Marlee as she milked him dry. The explosion seemed to shake him to the core.

After several moments, his grip on the scarf loosened and it fell back onto Marlee's chest. He looked down at her just as she extricated her mouth from around him.

She took another spoonful of ice cream in her mouth and swallowed it. Then another. She looked up at Declan and smiled.

"You know, women would do this much more frequently if there was always ice cream attached. No pun intended."

Declan reached for her, pulled her up, and kissed her

deeply. His tongue dove deep into her waiting mouth. She tangled her tongue with his, sucking it softly as she had just done to a different appendage.

She tasted ice cream and Declan and she wasn't sure which was sweeter.

Chapter 12

Thursday morning their work at the studio went smoothly. Declan taped his same spiel again, with new scores that Marlee got online. His hand usage decreased until it was unnoticeable. She hadn't given him much other advice; she said he hadn't needed any. It was her saying that which led him to believe he could actually do this without making a fool of himself. Marlee wouldn't lie to him just to make him feel better. He wasn't even sure Marlee knew how to lie.

"You're perfect, Declan. You didn't really need my help. The professionals in New York would have caught the hand thing in a minute. You definitely got the short end of this partnership."

Knowing what she meant, but playing dumb, Declan said, "Oh, I don't know—seems to me I was on the receiving end last night in your kitchen." There was a devilish grin in his eyes, as there always was when he teased her. And he teased her a lot. He thought at first that he was shaking loose her buttoned-up veneer, and he was. But he'd soon realized that Marlee had a playful side all her own, and it didn't take much prodding from Declan to bring it out. His ego allowed him to think that he was the man who could bring it out most easily.

"Actually, if you want to get technical, I was the one who did the receiving."

He hardened with arousal as he thought about Marlee draining him dry. She was standing at the newscaster set, resting her great ass against the corner of the desk, her long legs (again covered in jeans, much to Declan's delight and Marlee's chagrin) stretched out and crossed at the ankles. Today she was wearing a maroon cardigan. Not as tight as yesterday's sweater, but the buttons held some possibilities.

She took his breath away. She had an effect on Declan that he'd never experienced before. Even when she wore her hair up with the severe suits, he was more attracted to her than any other woman. But when she was like this, all warm and fuzzy in jeans and a sweater, her auburn waves gently framing her oval face, it made Declan think about moving up his future's timetable.

Maybe he didn't have to know for sure what his future held before he pursued a long-term commitment. It wasn't like he was hurting for money and wouldn't be able to support a wife and kids. He would never be idle; he wasn't the type. And who was to say that even if he got the broadcasting gig he'd like it, or be good at it, and still want to be doing it in a couple of years? He could conceivably be going through a professional upheaval the rest of his life, trying several different things. Waiting until he had it all figured out would never work in that case. Besides, if he did go through a variety of choices, wouldn't it be better to have a supportive wife and children to come home to for balance?

He'd never played it safe on the field, so why was he doing so now? If his father's untimely death had taught him anything, it was to live each day to the fullest. He'd always thought he was doing just that; his life was plenty exciting. But living to the fullest was no longer about sports accolades and sex with pretty young things. Nearing forty, Declan knew he longed for a family like the one he grew up in. He could be hit by a drunk driver, like his father had, tomorrow. Did he really want to put off pursuing a family until his professional life was settled?

Especially when Marlee was in his life *now*. Did he want to take the chance of letting her go only to hope to meet someone else that he'd care about more in a few years? *Who are you kidding? You're never gonna meet someone you care about more than Marlee.*

The revelation shook him. Of course. It seemed so clear. He loved Marlee. Letting her go now would be like punting on first down—it made no sense.

Something seemed to shift inside Declan. He hadn't felt this sense of complete clarity since he'd thrown his first touchdown pass in Pop Warner football.

As swiftly as the warmth of his newfound feelings had come, they blew away again faster than the Boston winter winds across the Charles River. Marlee didn't love him. Seemed perfectly content with their one-week arrangement.

He had a few more days to make Marlee see the light, make her realize that they'd be good together. Either that, or he needed to get her out of his system entirely. He'd always been known to do his best work in the fourth quarter—they hadn't dubbed him the Comeback Kid for nothing.

He was determined to win her over, yet he had lost enough games at the buzzer in his lifetime to know nothing was a sure thing. If this didn't work out, and Marlee walked out of his life for good on Sunday, he'd have to accept that.

It was that thought—never seeing Marlee again after this week—that spawned his next actions. He'd want a piece of

Marlee with him always. It wouldn't be enough to take out her memory every now and then and polish it like the trophies that adorned the walls of his den. He knew he'd want to relive every nuance of Marlee, again and again, until he could regain his perspective. Years of watching and re-watching his losses had taught him this. Hell, he still pulled out the tapes of his rookie season on occasion and played them, dissecting his every movement, taking away the good and berating himself for the bad.

Declan was moving files to a flash drive to add to the one they'd made yesterday. He took a step back and aimed the camera at Marlee. It didn't take much movement, because the camera was already pointed in the set's direction from Declan's rehearsal.

"Marlee," he said softly. She looked at him, waiting for him to speak. "Okay if I turn this on?" He motioned to the camera.

"Do you want to do another run-through?" She started to rise from where she leaned against the corner of the desk, but stopped when he held up a hand.

"No. That's not what I want to record."

She shook her head a tiny bit, and pushed her glasses up her cute nose. "I'm all set for today, if you were thinking of recording me."

"I was thinking of recording…*us*." He said it with enough innuendo in his tone that she quickly caught on.

"Uh…that would be no." She was giving him a "come on, get real" look, but she also sat up just the tiniest bit, and ran a hand through her hair.

"Why not? Think about how much you like it when I talk dirty to you. Just think of this as one step further. We could watch it together later."

She shook her head again. He expected a hard no, but

instead she said, "The equipment stays here in the studio. How could we…"

He motioned to the pile of flash drives on the table that they'd brought. "We copy the file onto a drive, then we erase the file from the camera and the laptop. I erase, you double-check to make sure."

"I don't know. I've never done anything like that." She was looking at the camera and biting her lip. So damn sexy.

"Me neither. Listen. We do it. You take the flash drive with you, so you are in complete control of the file. I admit, I like the thought of having you…with me…after this week, but I don't want you wondering what happened to the flash drive."

"I have the flash drive. We erase it from the camera and laptop?"

Holy shit, she was going to say yes. His cock sprang to attention and he put his hand over the on button of the camera. "Absolutely. Yours to do with what you want. Take a hammer to it if that's what you want. But I warn you, I'll try to talk you into watching it together."

There. That. That was what got her. She wanted to watch it together. She covered her face with her hands, her loose hair falling forward. After a tiny squeal, she lifted her head and said, "Turn the camera on."

He flipped the switch. "You're sure?"

"I trust you," she said. To hear those words from her meant a lot to him. And he didn't want to do anything that she'd regret later.

"I can still turn it off."

She shook her head and said, "Come here, Declan." Her voice was husky and his cock sprang to full attention as he moved toward her.

Out of the blue, the thought that he'd have to do

something really special for Joey went through his mind. Maybe a trip somewhere nice and warm for him and Kathy. No expense was too much as a thank-you for the introduction to Marlee. Hell, maybe he and Marlee could even join Joey and Kathy on that trip.

The vision of Marlee lying on a Hawaiian beach, her toes dug into the sand, a bikini barely covering her spectacular breasts, made Declan stumble against the rise of the set as he approached Marlee. He nearly fell into her, but caught himself just in time.

"I thought you were known for your fancy footwork," she said, laughing. Her arms were still open, a reaction to catch him that he hadn't needed. She dropped them down to the desk beside her hips and uncrossed her legs, spreading them wider than necessary for a normal stance.

It was good that he'd stumbled. It had kind of taken the newness of the camera being on down a couple of notches.

He moved in between her open thighs, grabbed her waist, and lifted her so that she was sitting on the desk, her jean-clad thighs brushing his. He turned her as he lifted her so that she was now completely on the side of the desk, its entire length behind her.

"My footwork's only fancy when I'm trying to evade defenders. And darlin', I've spent all week trying *not* to evade you." His hands were still on her waist and he squeezed her. A little harder than he would have normally, but he'd come to know what Marlee liked, and she wasn't one for flowers and poetry when it came to sex. She liked hard touches and rough caresses, and she loved it when he talked dirty to her. Whenever she was on the edge, Declan knew saying something steamy in her ear would send her over.

And apparently she also liked the idea of being videotaped. The paradox of the conservative professor getting off on dirty talk greatly amused Declan. And turned him on. It was that thought that had tempted him to turn on the camera. If she liked hearing dirty sweet nothings, would she like the idea of watching what they were about to film? He couldn't wait find out.

Declan had never had sex on tape before. Lots of women had suggested it, of course, and he'd been attentive to the idea. Even going so far as letting them pull out their phones. Then he'd have a flash of the recording ending up in the hands of some tabloid TV show with some cheesy voice over along the lines of "star quarterback in the sack," and the idea would be hit with cold water, like the traditional dousing of coaches with Gatorade buckets.

Marlee wiggled against him. "Evade me, or invade me?"

"Evade. I've been trying real hard to *invade* you, haven't you noticed?"

"Oh yeah, I've noticed. You're pretty good at it, too."

He silently agreed. He'd been subtly trying to invade Marlee's heart since he'd realized how much alike they were, how, down the road, there could be a possible future for them. He thought he'd made some progress with her, but wasn't sure. His other invasion, this one not so subtle, had been purely physical, and had worked well.

She wrapped her arms around his neck and pulled him close. She brought her breasts to his chest and rubbed herself against him. Nuzzling his neck, she whispered what she wanted in Declan's ear and he hardened instantly. He moved his hands to her hips and slid her backside along the desk, angling her so the camera could capture them both. It would be mostly a profile shot, but it would capture all of Marlee's body, and her face as he made her climax, and that was what Declan wanted.

He wanted the raw, sensuous Marlee, the Marlee he

figured only he got to see. The Marlee that let all those inhibitions go when she was in his arms. He wanted that Marlee on tape, so he could have her forever. But more so she could see her the way he did.

She wrapped her legs around Declan's thighs, pressing his cock into her soft, ready body.

Declan stepped back so he could see Marlee's face. He wanted what she had just said to be out loud so the camera could pick up on it, not whispered into his neck, although that had felt pretty damn good.

"Say it again, Marlee. Tell me again."

She leaned her head in once more to whisper to Declan, but he moved his head back.

"No. Look at me and say it. Don't whisper it."

She looked over at the camera nervously, but he put a finger on her chin and turned her face back to look at him.

"Own it, Marlee." He was pushing her past her comfort zone and he knew it, but since the moment he'd seen her at the party in his home, in her suit with her hair up in that tight bun, he'd needed to let this Marlee out. He knew she was in there. He smelled it in the same way he could smell a surprise blitz. Instinct.

She swallowed her indecision and raised her chin. *That's my girl.* Her voice was clear and true, her green-gold eyes locked on his.

"Take me, Declan. Now. Here. Take me hard and fast."

It sent Declan into motion. And emotion. Having a woman want him was nothing new. But Marlee…Marlee, who was trying so hard not to see how good they were together.

"Oh yeah, baby, I will. Anything for you, Marlee. Any way you want it." His fingers were already undoing the buttons on her sweater. He brushed the sweater away and filled his hands with her breasts, causing the nipples to spill over the edge of her pink lacy bra. Marlee wore underwire bras, and in this position the wires held her breasts in place above the pushed-down cups, almost acting like more of a bustier than a bra. Declan thought he'd never seen anything more sexy.

He bent his head down and wound his tongue around a peachy nipple. It pebbled instantly and he moved to the other nipple, where he continued. When both nipples were standing at attention, he took one in his mouth and sucked on her. He then bit down on the nipple, gently, but with enough force for Marlee to feel it.

She gasped out and put her hands on Declan's waist, already reaching for his belt buckle. He could do this to her, bring her to a fever pitch almost instantly. His touch burned her ivory skin, and his voice made her weak.

All thoughts about the camera being on flew out of Declan's mind the second Marlee eased his zipper down and reached inside to wrap her fingers around his hard shaft.

AT DINNER THAT NIGHT, IT SEEMED BY MUTUAL SILENT agreement that they wouldn't talk about the tape. After their amazing lovemaking on the desk, they had done just what Declan had described to her. First they'd transferred the digital file to the laptop via a cable, then loaded the file onto a flash drive. They had then deleted the file from the camera and the laptop, double-checking.

He didn't want to put the drive with their others, but he had an irrational vision of someone breaking into the studio, selecting that exact flash drive, and him ending up on TMZ. She had taken a red Sharpie and made an "X" on their drive so they'd be able to easily discern which the tape of their incredible sex.

And it had been incredible. Hard and fast, just as Marlee

had requested. Declan had even thrown in a little rough when he sensed Marlee wanted it. And she did. Nothing that would physically hurt either of them—Declan was experienced enough to know pain from pleasure; he had encountered both on the field and in the bedroom.

Her willing and eager response—not to mention her trust —had humbled him. Even now, hours later, Marlee's skin still glowed as they sat in the restaurant and gazed at each other over the candlelit table.

They'd gone back to Gino's restaurant, the place they'd gone with Joey and Kathy on the night they'd met. Five nights did not normally leave room for nostalgia to grow, but it seemed to this night. They both had the same salads they had ordered that first night. Declan picked out a wonderful Chardonnay that they both enjoyed.

"Almost done?" he asked her. Their plates had been cleared away and they had both been nursing their wineglasses for the last ten minutes.

"I'M SORRY, AM I HOLDING YOU UP?" MARLEE HAD enjoyed the long, leisurely dinner, but now the thought that maybe Declan had somewhere he wanted to be entered her mind.

Of course he had somewhere he needed to be; she had monopolized his time for the last four days. How could she think that Declan would be content to just be with her, working in the studio during the days, spending the evenings cooking in her kitchen or going out for dinner like they were doing now, and then going to bed early, though not going to sleep until much later.

This was Declan Tate, for Pete's sake—the man was probably surrounded at all times by teammates or groupies or hangers-on of some sort. Being solely with her was probably killing him. Oh, she knew he enjoyed sex with her—you couldn't fake the kind of body-racking orgasms that Declan had with her. In her. On her. But to be with her, just her, twenty-four/seven had to be getting to him.

Odd—it wasn't getting to her, and she was used to spending the majority of her time alone. Still, that must be why Declan seemed in a rush to end their dinner; he had other plans for the evening.

"You're not holding me up. I just want to get you home so I can hold *you* up…like against a wall, or maybe another door." His voice was low, almost a whisper, even though the restaurant wasn't crowded and Gino had again placed them in a secluded corner, and all the tables that surrounded them were empty.

A breath of…relief?…went through Marlee. He wasn't rushing off to be somewhere else, he was in a hurry to be alone…with her. "Tempting as that is, I need to go to the store."

"No you don't. I bought two boxes of condoms, and we still have a couple left from the first box."

She laughed at his assumption. "Of course you'd think that was the only staple we'd need."

"Well, isn't it? What more do you need, Marlee? Seems to me you've been pretty satisfied with what I've offered up." He leaned close, pinned her with his gaze, and turned on that sexy drawl. "And I'm not talking about my pesto sauce."

That voice, what it did to her. And he knew it. It was low and sexy, almost as gravelly as it became when he was inside her, telling her how much he wanted her. Just the memory made Marlee's insides tingle.

As did the thought that they'd captured it all on on video. She still couldn't believe she'd done it. And if she was honest with herself…she had been aroused by the idea of the running camera while Declan took her on the desk.

She shook her head, trying to break free of the exciting memory.

"True as that may be, I still need to go to the store. Yes, you can give me everything I want, Declan, but I'm having my family over for dinner tomorrow night, and I'd rather you not be offering any of *that* to my sisters."

"I don't know, do your sisters look like you?" he teased.

"They're much prettier, but my brothers-in-law keep them well satisfied."

"There's well satisfied, and then there's Tate satisfied, and darlin', I know you know the difference." He leaned back in the booth, putting both hands behind his head, playing the proud peacock.

Marlee laughed. "You're not going to refer to yourself in the third person, are you?"

"Declan wouldn't do that, he's too humble for that."

"Real humble. Tate satisfied. As if." She smiled, but knew there was some truth to Declan's jest. She'd been more satisfied with Declan in just a few days than in relationships with other men that had lasted several months, some of them years. And so much more so than Justin Jones.

She'd never achieved this level of intimacy with any other man, hadn't even come close to being as uninhibited with another lover. She surmised that Declan's physical dominance over every other man she'd known was the reason, but she had an inkling that she was so free with Declan because, deep down, she knew it wouldn't last past Sunday. An all-or-nothing feeling that allowed her to play out her natural desires. Desires she'd never even realized she had before meeting Declan.

"Okay, sorry. Back to the subject at hand. Groceries. Your

family. Tomorrow night. What am I cooking? I assume you want the best chef in the house to cook for such special guests."

She didn't miss a beat with her comeback. "That's right, I do, so I'll be cooking. I'm making vegetable lasagna."

They both laughed, enjoying the banter, feeling more clever than they actually were, but too sated in the aftermath of their carnal mating on the desk to care.

"Lasagna? A bit prosaic, don't you think?"

"Don't forget, I'll be serving my nieces and nephews as well. Haute cuisine is a little hard to get past a four-year-old's palate. I've finally gotten so the fifteen-year-old won't totally turn his nose up at the idea of vegetarian lasagna."

"The fifteen-year-old, that would be Captain Hook?"

It took her a second to catch his meaning, and then she was impressed that he would remember the picture and her explanation of Hook's current age. Maybe he hadn't been just filling time between sex sessions with idle chitchat. Maybe he really had wanted to get to know her.

They'd spent hours in bed as they came down from their incredible highs, talking and sharing childhood stories. Marlee had treasured those times, but she wasn't sure that Declan had been as rapt as she. After all, was a man really listening to a woman speak when he had one hand caressing her breast, and the other buried deep between her legs? Apparently Declan had been.

She nodded to his assumption of her nephew's identity.

"Let me make sure I remember. Susan is the oldest. Husband is Charlie. Brent—or Hook, as I call him—is fifteen, Heather is ten, and Matt is eight, right?" At Marlee's stunned nod, Declan continued, "Then there's Linda and Larry. Cute, by the way, the alliterative names. And their Graham is eight, same as Matt, and Grace is four. Is your brother Patrick coming too?"

A flabbergasted Marlee shook her head. "No, he's in New York. How did you know all that?"

He shrugged, as if the answer was obvious. "You told me. The other night in bed. When we were talking about our families."

"Okay, let me rephrase. How did you *remember* all that?"

"I told you all about my family. Could you tell me their names and approximate ages?"

Marlee scanned her brain. "Yes, I could."

"Then why do you assume that I wouldn't be able to do the same? Because I'm a guy?" Declan's eyes narrowed on Marlee. "Or because I'm a jock?"

"Neither. It's because you normally had your hands all over my body while we were having those discussions."

"That's the beauty of my talent, Marlee. I can work my crotch and my cranium at the same time."

She smiled at him. Oh yes, she did know how well he worked his crotch.

"Okay, vegetarian lasagna it is. You're in luck—it's another one of my specialties."

"Oh. You'll be there? Tomorrow night? For dinner with my family?" She saw a flash of something in his eyes, but she couldn't quite read it.

"I had intended on being there. But if you don't want me to meet your family…"

"It's not that. This was planned weeks ago, because I'd be leaving soon and wouldn't see them for a while. I just thought that maybe you'd rather not be inundated with my family. I'd love for you to meet them, Declan, but please don't feel it's necessary."

He nodded. "Good. I'd like to meet them too. It'll be fun.

Okay. So, a stop at the grocery store on the way home. And then straight to bed for you, little girl. It must be way past your bedtime."

It was seven in the evening. Even if they spent an inordinate amount of time at the store, they'd be home by nine.

"Oh yes, way past my bedtime," she said.

Chapter 13

F riday morning at the studio, Marlee ran through her lecture with the basketball jargon that Declan had written for her substituted in for the football terms. It went smoothly. She taped the entire lecture one last time, but felt confident that she knew the terms and, more importantly, what they meant and that they enhanced her message.

She also played the videotape for Declan that she used to open her lecture. She had an advanced telecom class at BC do it for her. It contained footage from all over the world of poor public speakers interspersed with shots of text, tweets, and Facebook posts filled with emoticons and poor abbreviations. All edited together, it demonstrated the breakdown of communication and its effects on poor speech and public speaking. Sadly, it was all too easy to find footage to include in the montage. The tape ended with a college football player being barely understandable while being interviewed, with "huh," "and, like," and "I was all" being the mainstays of his answers.

That was where she got the idea to start her talk with a

football analogy coming on the heels of the athlete's footage. It would smoothly segue into her opening lines and the football metaphors she had sprinkled throughout.

She'd seen the montage before, of course, but enjoyed watching it again as she showed it to Declan.

DECLAN DID ONE MORE TAPE OF HIMSELF, WHICH HE'D bring, along with all the others, with him to New York. He, too, seemed confident with where he stood. He still had doubts about his future, but they weren't based in insecurities about his ability to be comfortable in front of the camera. He had Marlee to thank for that. Even just watching how she handled herself when she did her lecture gave him ideas of things he'd like to try.

The way she'd pause after a particularly important thought. The minimal gestures she made, so that when she did it brought great emphasis. He'd learned a lot from her. He felt at ease now. About that, anyway.

The unknowns of his future still loomed heavily before him. The whole broadcasting thing still didn't sit one hundred percent right with him. It felt…forced, somehow. It was a natural progression for former players, particularly quarterbacks, to go into broadcasting, but it had never really been in Declan's plans. Probably because before last Sunday, Declan hadn't given any thought to the day after he'd step off the field for the last time. He would never even discuss it when his agent or others would bring it up, preferring to concentrate on the career at hand—winning games.

Now, faced with the rest of his life in front of him, he had decided to give this option his attention first. There were other possibilities. Things that would still keep him in contact with football. The Pumas front office had told him there would always be a place with them, perhaps as a scout. Declan knew that the offer, real as it was, was made out of loyalty, and he wouldn't take an offer out of allegiance alone.

There was coaching. The problem with a superstar becoming a head coach was that his notoriety often got in the way of being able to lead the team.

No, broadcasting was his best shot at a future. And, even though he wasn't completely sold on the idea, being a fierce competitor, Declan wanted to excel at this as he had in his previous vocation.

He told Marlee all of this as they sat in the large chairs from the talk show set. They had the TV cart pointed at them, having just watched the tape of Declan's morning session.

"I'm glad if you think working together helped, Declan…"

"Somehow I feel there's a 'but' that goes with that."

Their chairs were close, side by side, but turned toward each other so Declan and Marlee were facing each other. Declan was once again in a knit shirt and jeans. Marlee was adamant that she'd been casual long enough and had donned another suit for today's work. At least this one had a skirt instead of slacks, so he could see some of her wondrous legs.

"There is, I guess. From all that you've just said…I don't know…it just seems like you're only doing this audition because you think that's what ex-quarterbacks do, not because you have any real interest in it."

"I guess that's true. Or partially true, anyway. I should probably take a year off and think about it all." Marlee seemed to agree with that and was nodding, so Declan added, "But my agent says I have to strike while the iron's hot. That I'm a name right now and I should capitalize on that."

"That makes sense." Her voice was soft, but lacked conviction. "I guess I don't know what to tell you. Obviously

I'd like you to be happy. It just doesn't seem like the idea of this is exciting to you."

"Exciting? No. But it's a way to stay in the game while maintaining some dignity. That's important to me, Marlee. I'm scared to death that in a year I'll miss it so much I'll come out of retirement and make a fool of myself. Or that I'll spend all my time on the golf course betting on closest to the pin with CEOs of major corporations who want to say they golfed with Declan Tate."

"Granted, I don't know you very well, Declan, but—"

He didn't let her finish her thought, but leaned forward and took her hands. "No. You haven't known me for very *long*. It's not the same thing. You do know me well. So well it scares you just a little, doesn't it?"

As Marlee sat in silence, unable—or unwilling—to answer him, Declan saw his shot and decided to take it. He wanted to show her how it could be for them for more than just this week. He wanted her to know what they could be for…a lifetime?

He'd been aware of his growing feelings all through the week, but now it hit him with such clarity that it almost physically pushed him back in his chair.

He was in love with Marlee. He would always be in love with Marlee. And she loved him too. He was certain of it. She just wouldn't allow herself to see it. To see them. Together. Long term. He leaned toward her, wanting to make love to her. Make love. Not just have incredible sex.

She put a hand on his chest, stopping him. Looking him in the eye, she whispered, "Turn on the camera."

She didn't have to tell him twice.

MARLEE FELT A LITTLE OFF-KILTER. DECLAN HAD SUCKER-punched her with his comment about her knowing him and being afraid of it. Then he'd gotten this passionate look in his eyes and he'd leaned in to kiss her. Different from the other passionate looks he'd given her all week.

Declan seemed determined to make her come to terms with her feelings about him, yet he had never mentioned his to her. Oh, pillow talk, sure. How much he wanted her, how hot she made him. All in the throes of passion. But outside of bed? Marlee replayed all their conversations. Lots of talk about how alike they were. But nothing about how he *felt* about her.

He returned to his chair after turning on the camera, but didn't make another move toward her, just watched her.

She couldn't believe it yesterday when she'd agreed to being filmed. She also couldn't believe how much hotter it had made the whole thing. And they'd been plenty hot all week.

And she trusted Declan. Knew he would never show the tape to anyone. Justin had begged her to let him film them together, but she'd always said no. Maybe some part of her instinctively knew she shouldn't trust Justin. Obviously she trusted Declan more than any man she'd ever been with.

She lifted her hands to her head to squeeze her temples and hopefully squeeze out her thoughts. Declan caught her hands in his. He gave a gentle tug to them, to pull Marlee out of her chair and onto his lap.

His hard body was a safe haven for her. This was what she needed. To make love to Declan. To let her body feel, instead of letting her mind run. To have him take her as swiftly and roughly as he had yesterday. To blot out the aching that had begun in her heart. Had begun the first night she met Declan and knew there couldn't possibly be any future for them. It had been easy to block it out with her other senses dancing all week long. Another slam-bam session with Declan would have her body tingling so strongly her heart wouldn't dare speak up.

She put an arm around his neck and leaned her body into his. She became soft and pliant the second he wrapped his broad arm around her waist. His other arm draped across her knees and his hand played with the hem of her skirt that was just above her knees.

She kicked off her shoes and silently applauded her decision to wear a skirt today. She'd also had the forethought to wear thigh-high silk stockings instead of pantyhose. She didn't assume they'd make love today at the studio, but their intense coupling yesterday on the desk, and knowing they had a very light workday ahead of them, made her prepare for the possibility.

It was the Boy Scouts' motto to be prepared, but Marlee tried to make it her credo as well. One quick movement to get her panties off and she could have Declan pounding inside her, taking her to another fantastic high.

She lifted her free hand to his zipper, having to shift her weight to her outside hip because she was pressed so tightly to Declan that she needed room to get to her destination. Declan's cock. She could feel him becoming erect under her bottom and she squirmed to feel him grow. She tugged on the back of his neck, sending him a silent message of what she needed.

Declan.

Her hand became more forceful against his neck, kneading the strong muscles, increasing the pressure as her need built.

Her other hand was pulling at his shirt, trying to free it from his jeans so she'd have better access to him. Her fingers tangled in the cloth, slowing her down, and her urgency manifested itself in a moan that came from deep in her chest and was filled with sorrow, passion, and need.

He grabbed her hand and held it in his own, away from him, back to rest on her knee. It was not done as a sexy maneuver; in fact, they more resembled a child on Santa's lap than the carnal position she was craving.

"Sshh, baby, we'll get there, but we need to slow down," he said, his voice low due to his arousal. He hadn't whispered in the seductive pitch that made her wild, nor did he use that commanding voice that made her obey his every word while she rose to new heights. No, he kept his voice level and firm, seemingly wanting her to know the difference.

And she did. Her head jerked up from where she was just about to bite his neck to spur him on. "Huh?" She had an astounding vocabulary, but "huh" was all her muddled mind could come up with.

"Let's slow down, Marlee." His left hand gently stroked her waist where he held her, and his right hand let go of hers and began to softly caress her knees and calves. He blanketed light kisses on her neck, bare to him with her hair back again in its regular bun.

This was different. She could feel the difference in him. Was it for the camera? She didn't think so; he hadn't been different yesterday.

He was doing the sweetest things to her neck.

She didn't want sweet. Not now, and certainly not with Declan. Sweet and tender with Declan would be her downfall. It was all she could do to keep this whole encounter at fling level, to not let her consciousness confront the reality that she and Declan were so much alike, had so much in common, could be so good together. If she registered that truth, there'd be no hope for her, and when Declan walked out of her life on Sunday, she'd be devastated.

She waited for the soft kisses to turn to nips and bites on her sensitive skin, for his hand to suddenly leave her knee and plunge deep under her skirt with his fingers searching, but neither happened.

Her body tensed with this new development. He wanted to go slow? Just when she needed the mind numbing that down-and-dirty sex with Declan always brought her? Uhhh… no. She'd bring him back to the fold. And she knew how to do it. Declan could bring her to fever pitch with his words, but she had noticed what her verbal responses did to him. Tit for tat.

She pulled her head back, gripped the back of his neck tightly, and forced him to leave her neck and meet her gaze. She brought her lips crashing to his, her tongue plunging into his mouth, seeking out the warm moistness of his. She tangled with it for a few seconds, then drew her head back as abruptly as she had brought them together. She had just wanted to tease, to taste, to get his attention, and now she'd get him back on track. Her eyes locked on his once more.

"No. Not slow, Declan. I want you inside me. Hard. Deep. Fast." She waited a moment for her words to sink in. She saw his pupils dilate, his eyes going near black, the jade green that she loved to gaze at nearly eclipsed. His erection jumped underneath her and she ground her bottom into him, eliciting a hard moan from deep in his throat. But he kept his hands quiet on her, his touch still soft, barely there. He seemed to be fighting some internal battle, and Marlee knew she needed to pull out the big guns.

"Give me your cock, Declan. Now. I want your cock inside me."

She had never spoken so blatantly, so boldly, and she was shocked that the words hadn't stuttered out, or that she hadn't choked on them. No, they seemed to roll out, with a conviction she hadn't even realized was inside her. Not even as much as a blush rose to her cheeks. The words were true. It was what she wanted, and that alone was what allowed her eyes to never waver from Declan's as she made her request.

She knew the incongruity of such words coming from her conservative, reserved, seemingly repressed mouth was a thrill to Declan. The thought that he could make the professor talk dirty excited him. Truth was, it was as titillating to her as it was to him, and she suspected Declan knew that also.

Chapter 14

To not take Marlee up on her desire was harder for Declan than remaining in the pocket with a 350-pound linebacker bearing down on him. In those situations, he had to stick to his plan and rely on his faith that one of his own linemen would come out of nowhere and take out the threat.

Just like that scenario, Declan now had to have faith that his plan of slow, tender lovemaking would allow Marlee and him to make it to the end zone. For him to make the ultimate score. Making Marlee admit she loved Declan as much as he loved her.

"It'll happen, baby, all in good time." His voice was gentle and he kept contact with her eyes. He tried to keep his growing arousal out of his voice, wanted it to have a calming effect on her, so unlike what he normally tried to evoke from her with his words and tone. "I need to touch you first, Marlee. I need to see you, all that sweet, soft, white skin you have underneath this suit."

He slowly undid the buttons to her suit jacket. There were only three, but he paused after each one to place a tender kiss on her cheek, her eyes, her nose. He slid the jacket off of her and dropped it to the carpeted floor of the set beside the chair.

Her blouse was satin, a collarless confection in a deep, dusty rose color. Declan couldn't help thinking that the color of her top was hauntingly reminiscent of Marlee's nipples when he had sucked them for a long period of time.

He brushed the thought from his mind. If he was going to block out Marlee's urgency, both in words and actions, he had to be able to rein in his own ruminations or she'd have her way and it would be over in a matter of minutes.

The blouse had several pearly buttons, and Declan once again paused after he undid each one for a kiss. This time they were all aimed at Marlee's mouth.

When she saw where his aim was headed, she licked her lips in anticipation of some of their soul-deep, mouth-grinding kisses, but again he kept her off guard. Instead, his lips barely touched hers. His mouth was soft and warm as it grazed over Marlee's, never daring to enter, only to entice. Button. Brush of lips. Button. Brush of lips. He was taking his time and she was losing her mind. And he liked it.

She tried again to force him to her, tugging at his neck, trying to invade his mouth with her tongue, but he was too strong for her. His strength was in the gentleness of his actions, the sweetness of his kisses, the delicate way his hand stroked her knees. His hand stayed there, never daring to rise to her heat.

"Mmmm. Isn't this nice? You'll see, baby. My way this time. It'll be good, Marlee. Just enjoy the ride."

Her head dropped back just as he undid her last button, and Declan knew that he'd chosen the right game plan. Her face showed it all. Her arousal was plain—the parting of her lips, the eyes open only to slits, the heat creeping up her pale neck.

But it was different. She was feeling, and, more importantly, she was thinking. It was deeper. Taking her there slowly was allowing her to grasp the emotions as they happened, not become overwhelmed with them, as it was when they normally came together so quickly.

He took off her blouse and set it on top of her jacket. Her lacy peach bra was similar to the one the first time Declan had seen her this way. Had it only been five days ago? It seemed like an eternity. He couldn't remember a time before Marlee, any other woman before Marlee. Her breasts swelled above the cups of her bra, and he had to take another glance at her passion-filled face to reinforce his decision to go slow with her.

"Marlee, God, you're so beautiful like this." She slowly lifted her head where it had been arched and looked into his eyes. "Your breasts, so milky white; even now your nipples are hardening, waiting for my touch. The arousal, the anticipation, it's climbing your neck, your sexy, classy neck, and resting in that incredible face. You're burning up, Marlee."

She was, she had flushed beyond pink.

"Put out the fire, Declan, please." She reached behind her, undid her bra, and dropped it to the floor. She placed her hands under her breasts and held them up to Declan, offering herself to him, daring him to take her, begging him to.

He slightly raised the arm that had been around Marlee's waist so that it was in the middle of her back and then pushed up, forcing her to arch her back.

God, what a vision. Marlee's hands on herself, giving herself to him.

"Lie back, Marlee."

The chairs were slightly oversized and the arms were overstuffed, acting more like side pillows than arms of a chair. Marlee's head came to rest on the outside of it, just slightly hanging over the edge. Her back was supported by the upholstery of the arm and her bottom was still in Declan's lap. It was a natural motion for her body when Declan placed his right hand under her knees and unbent her legs, draping them over the other arm of the chair.

His hand along her back slid down to undo the button and zipper at the back of her skirt, and she lifted her hips so he could shimmy her skirt down, off her legs to join all her other clothes.

She lay across him, naked except for her peach satin panties and her thigh-high stockings. The elastic band at the top of the stockings was edged with peach lace. Declan's gaze traveled up her sinewy legs, over the panties that seemed to be growing darker with her moistness, along her firm tummy and farther up. Her hands were still under her breasts in silent offering. His eyes continued along the slender column of her graceful neck, to her mouth, which seemed to tremble ever so slightly, and to her eyes.

Behind her ever-present glasses, her bewitching eyes met his. They had been on him the whole time. They were filled with desire and passion and a need in her that Declan knew only he could fill.

He began mentally running over all his stats, beginning with his rookie season, in his head. It was the only way he knew to make this last. Having Marlee look at him like that, with such rocking emotion, he had to let his mind wander or he'd have her on the floor, buried in her to the hilt, in a matter of seconds.

"God, Marlee, you're like a feast, all laid out in front of me. A bunch of tasty delights." His eyes roved hungrily over her entire body again. "Let's see, what do I nibble on first?" He heard the hitch in her breath and then the pattern changed, deeper and faster breaths, her breasts rising where she still held them up for him.

He took her hands in his and led them away from her breasts. "No. I won't let you cheat and get there quicker. Only I get to touch you today. Only me. No one else."

Ever. He wanted to add it, to feel her out, to start planting seeds, but he'd insisted on going slow with her, so he figured that included his end too.

He placed her arms over her head so that her forearms and hands dangled over the side of the chair. The position also caused her breasts to push farther into the air, and there was no way Declan could deny them, or himself, pleasure any longer.

He didn't have to lean down far; the high upholstery of the chair allowed Marlee's glorious body to be only inches from Declan. He put his face to her chest and placed a chaste kiss on Marlee's heart, silently wishing that he would be touching it, on many levels, beyond today.

He let his lips glide down from her heart over the swell of her breast. His tongue followed the trail his lips blazed until he arrived at her nipple, already spear-like in its intensity. He circled her taut peak with his rough tongue and watched as her whole breast tightened and flushed. He held her other breast and he began gently playing with the nipple. His mouth, needing more than just a taste of her sweetness, took her in and began to tenderly suck. He knew he would never taste anything as delicious as Marlee if he lived to be a hundred.

She arched her back when he began to suckle her. She ground her bottom into Declan's hard erection. She was trying to spur him on, her need apparent as she roughly brushed her thighs together. The movement pulled Declan out of idolatry of her breasts and he backed off, taking both his hand and mouth from her glistening globes.

He placed a hand on her thighs to still her. "No, baby.

That's a form of touching yourself. No cheating. Like I said, only me, Marlee. Only *me* touching you."

Her forearms covered her eyes, her wrists crossed, and the palms of her hands were facing the ceiling, like she was trying to block out the world. Declan could only see pieces of her tortoiseshell frames peeking out. But he could see her mouth. See how heavily she was breathing. See her tongue dart out to wet her lips, which had suddenly gone dry. See her teeth grab and gnaw her bottom lip as the sensations overwhelmed her.

His left hand edged under her and began stroking the soft skin of her lower back. His fingers skimmed the waistband of her panties. Back and forth across the elastic, sometimes dipping in against the soft skin of her bottom, sometimes taking his fingers away completely. He kept the rhythm of the sweeping the same, but changed up the destination of his fingers to keep her guessing.

The touches were light for a reason, and Declan could see it was working. Though she had closed her eyes, there was no way to mask the fact that emotions were crashing through Marlee Reeves. Her mouth pursed, almost as if she were in pain, and her teeth pulled on her lower lip. The gentle caresses were getting to her.

While he continued with his left hand at her back, he let his right hand come to rest on the front of her panties, the palm of his hand cupping her mound, his fingers nearly touching her belly button. The contact was so weightless that Marlee raised her head and opened her eyes, almost as if to see if Declan had really finally touched her or if her aching body had needed the touch so much she had imagined it.

Declan could read her mind. "Yes, Marlee, it's me touching you. Do you like that?" As he knew she would, Marlee nodded. She began to open her mouth to answer, but Declan cut her off. "Good. Lie back. Close your eyes, let me touch you like you want…only me, Marlee…only me touching you."

Without moving the ball or palm of his hand, his fingers skimmed the waistband of her panties, spanning from one hipbone to the other. His left hand, at her back, was doing the same thing on her other side, and he knew that Marlee expected him to grab both sides and quickly slide the panties off her. Or even rip them off her, as he'd done their first night together.

But Declan didn't want to give Marlee what she expected. He needed to keep her off-kilter. Their pattern needed to change. He wasn't sure in what convoluted thought process he had correlated slow lovemaking with a breakthrough of Marlee's feelings for him, but the equation was there and he couldn't shake it. He knew it was irrational, but he was now single-minded in his quest.

He moved his hand down from her mound to her thigh. He stroked the soft skin that encased the strong muscles and once again thought about his underestimation of yoga. God, but it did great things to Marlee's legs.

He slowly edged his hand down until the tips of his fingers were at the elastic of the leg entrance of her panties. The ball of his hands pressed down on her thigh, kneading the muscles, as he rubbed it back and forth. The entry of his fingers into her panties at the juncture of her thigh was seamless, and again Marlee began to raise her head to see if Declan had really touched her, the sensation was so feathery.

"Lie back, Marlee." His tone was slightly more forceful this time, and she laid her head back and met his eyes. "Close your eyes. Just feel me, Marlee. You don't need to see my hands on you, you can feel me. Can't you?" He watched her face and saw the slow, almost imperceptible nod. "That's right. Just feel me touching you. Only me, Marlee."

"Declan. Declan…I…I need…"

"I know what you need. I'll get you there." His fingers moved further in, spreading her slick folds, feeling her throbbing heat, her crying need. Just a few sleek strokes was all it would take to shatter her.

He could tell it wasn't what she wanted. Oh, she wanted him all right, but not this way. She began to struggle in his lap, fighting her way to sit up. Reading her movement as desperation for release, he began to stroke her faster while cooing sweet words to her.

"Declan, no, let me up, let me up."

The words made him release his hold on her, taking his hand from her panties and pushing her up at the back with his other hand. Had he hurt her? Pushed her too far?

"I need you, Declan. I need you to be inside me when I come. Please." She held his face as she spoke, and before he could register her words she had swung herself around so that she was straddling him. She let go of his face and began tugging at his shirt.

He helped her with his shirt, taking over getting it off and to the floor while her attention came to rest upon his jeans. She slid herself back along his thighs so there was room for her hands to start undoing his fly. That done, she eased his jutting penis out of his jeans and underwear. She clasped him and began to stroke his length as she rubbed her breasts against his chest. His coarse chest hair scraped against her tender nipples, eliciting moans from them both.

He had tried to go slow with her, he really had. And, honestly, this was probably the most drawn out their lovemaking had been all week. Good thing, because Declan couldn't stand it any longer. He rocked to one hip to get a condom out of his wallet, and even that small motion seemed to nearly send Marlee over. She was so ready. He rolled the condom on and took her hand in his, then wrapped her fingers around his cock. "Guide me to you. Put me inside you."

He left her hand covering him and took both his hands to her face. He lifted her head until they were eye level. A look of sweet anticipation was swathed across Marlee's oval face. "Open your eyes, Marlee. Look at me while you take me in. Take all of me."

She opened her eyes as she pushed the fabric of her panties aside, not even taking the time to remove them, and lowered herself on to Declan. She gasped at the fullness, the depth. He growled at the tenderness, at the shining light that was behind Marlee's green-gold eyes.

Her glasses had slid down her nose, and Declan reached around from the side of her head and pushed them back into place, then leaned forward and placed a soft kiss on the top of her nose. Small tears swept down her face and Declan brushed them aside with the pad of his thumb, still holding her face in his hands.

She came down hard once again, and Declan raised his hips up to meet her, and they both spiraled out of control. It seemed to go on forever, rippling and shuddering, gasps and moans, neither knowing which sound came from whom, nor did they care.

The entire time, they never took their eyes off of each other. It was if they were looking into each other's souls.

Only them.

Chapter 15

As Marlee slowly dressed, she was only vaguely aware of her surroundings. She was still dazed by what she and Declan had just experienced together. Nothing like that had ever happened to her. Her arms seemed to be barely working as she put her bra back on. She was surprised to find that her legs would hold her weight as she stood to gather the rest of her clothes. Her body was liquid, and she felt as though at any minute someone would cut the strings that held her up and she would melt to the floor like the Wicked Witch of the West when doused with water.

She continued to dress, but her eyes were drawn to Declan. It seemed as though she was always drawn to Declan.

Only me, Marlee.

He was moving around the room, putting himself back together, pulling his shirt over his head, covering up his incredible back and shoulders. As he pulled his jeans tight to refasten them, the denim flexed across his spectacular behind and Marlee nearly swallowed her tongue.

It was nothing new, this strong effect having sex with Declan had on her. But it was different this time.

Only me.

The sex had gone to another level, and Marlee had been sure that there was no level more intense than the one they'd been at all week. She'd been wrong.

This was more than sex. More than just a physical mating. Thoughts and words of definition flicked through her mind, but she had no desire to pinpoint anything right now. Not when she could just stand here and watch Declan.

For the first time in her life, she regretted that she didn't follow sports. What a treat it would have been to watch Declan Tate in action these past years. The man could move. Her newly found, and very limited, football knowledge jumped to action, and she imagined Declan in those form-hugging tight pants football players wore, moving quickly to evade tacklers.

For a big guy (and Marlee now knew that compared to his teammates Declan was tiny, but still, a big guy by normal standards), he could move with the ease and stealth of a panther. Or a Puma. He was in absolute control of his body at all times. Even when they were at their most passionate peak, Marlee sensed that Declan could rein himself in at a moment's notice. It must have taken him years to gain that self-awareness, and lucky her got to benefit from all that hard work.

For one more day. The thought came at her out of nowhere but refused to leave. It pulled up a chair and settled in, ready to pipe up the second Marlee would think about Declan in any context beyond Sunday. The guest that would not leave.

Party pooper.

Marlee's eyes followed him, but her thoughts were not on his actions, but on the way his body moved. With purpose.

He was like that when they'd have sex—at least in their past sessions, his movements sure and knowing, no extra activity, no fuss, just a goal in sight and the most expedient way of getting there. This time there seemed to be more flourish, more…emotion, but his goal had been as clear cut as before.

What had he called it when he explained football? Oh yes. Moving the ball down the field. That was how he'd summed up his job one night while they had lain in bed exhausted. He had joked about writing his résumé and how his objective for the past sixteen years had been to simply move the ball.

He was gathering up their things at the table and turned the camera off, which broke Marlee from her reverie. She was slipping on the last of her clothes back on, and she checked her watch. Four o'clock.

They had planned on quitting early today so they would have lots of time to play and experiment in the kitchen before her family arrived at seven. Declan wanted to make his mother's famous chocolate chip cookie recipe for dessert.

They had originally thought they wanted to leave around two, but Marlee wouldn't have given up the past two hours even if she had to serve her family pizza from the nearest delivery place and a bag of Oreos. In fact, the kids would probably prefer that.

They'd still be okay, time-wise, if they got a move on now.

She went to the table and helped Declan do the same file-transfer-and-erase procedure that they'd done yesterday. As she handed him the flash drive with the red X on it to add their newest file to, she said, a tiny bit testily, "Come on. Let's get a move on. Let's see that Tate speed. We're going to have my family waiting till midnight to eat if we don't get going."

DECLAN SHOULD HAVE REALIZED THAT HE'D PUSHED Marlee as far as she could go without breaking in one day. And he didn't want her breaking. It was a start. Hell, it was more than a start; she had come apart in his arms while never taking her beautiful eyes from his. And even though she was now embarrassed and double-checking that he had erased their tape from the camera, she smiled at Declan to let him know she hadn't meant anything by her tone.

He could live with that. Hell yeah, he could live with that. And tonight he'd work on her family. Then tomorrow he'd break down the rest of her barriers by watching their tape together.

On Sunday, he'd be down to his two-minute drill. That was his specialty. He'd won more games in the last two minutes in his career than he cared to count. They had dubbed him the Comeback Kid, and the nomenclature had stuck even though he was hardly a kid anymore. But Comeback Middle-Aged Man didn't have much of a ring to it.

They took one last glance around to make sure they hadn't forgotten anything as they headed for the door. Marlee's eyes came to rest on the upholstered chairs, and Declan's eyes came to rest on Marlee. She sensed Declan's gaze and ducked her head in a soft smile, remembering. She met his eyes, and as though it were contagious, her smile passed on to Declan. He placed his hand possessively on her neck and they left the studio.

Their studio. A place where they had shared secrets and intimacies, where they had worked on their professional lives and had dove into the personal realm as well. Where she had trusted him enough to allow their lovemaking to be recorded. Where she had *asked* to have it recorded.

It had only been five days, only four of which they'd been there together, and yet it seemed like they had been together for years.

Unwilling to break their contact, they walked down the

hallway of the building with his hand on his neck. There was a drop box outside of an advisor's office where Marlee would place the studio keys now that she was done with them.

The building was quiet, nearly deserted. The students were still on break. The new semester not starting for two more weeks.

She broke from Declan to put the keys in the drop box, and they turned to leave the building. As they walked to the doors, he took Marlee's hand in his and she gave it a gentle squeeze. She was looking at him, smiling at him, so that she didn't see the man who was entering the building some ten yards in front of them. The man brushed the snow from his shoulders and recognized Marlee immediately.

"Professor Reeves? Marlee?"

The man was bundled up in a long overcoat, but Declan could tell just by the look of him, with a pipe in his mouth and a fedora (with a feather in it, no less!), that this was an academic colleague of Marlee's. Declan would bet one of his Super Bowl rings that underneath that top coat, the guy's jacket had suede elbow patches.

Marlee looked up, and as she recognized the approaching man she simultaneously dropped her hand from Declan's. Oh, she was subtle about it, pretending she needed the hand free to readjust her satchel strap on her shoulder and then pushing her glasses up her nose, but she hadn't fooled Declan.

She didn't want this man to see her holding hands with him. Who was this guy? A former lover? A *current* lover? The thought pissed Declan off, and he almost snatched her hand back, but he didn't. He had pushed her far enough for today.

Besides, there was no way the Marlee he'd gotten to know so well this week would be currently seeing someone while she and Declan were together. She was definitely the monogamous type. It didn't even surprise Declan to discover that he was too. At least with Marlee.

"Professor Curtis. How are you?" They had reached one another and the three stood facing each other. Marlee turned her body to form more of a semi-circle rather than standing side by side with Declan. The deft body language was not lost on him.

"I'm fine, thank you. And yourself?" the man answered. The sentiment was directed at Marlee, but he was looking at Declan.

"Fine. Fine." Her voice was just a touch shrill. Marlee was never shrill. Declan wondered again if this was a former lover. Or maybe it was her boss, come to check up on her in the studio? Good thing the guy hadn't arrived a half-hour earlier.

"What brings you to this building?" His eyes didn't leave Declan's.

"I've been using the video studio this week, preparing my speech." She made some kind of movement to start out of the building, but was thwarted by the continued conversation of Professor Curtis.

"That's right, your tour starts next week, doesn't it? Well, we'll certainly miss you around the Communications Department this semester. Think of us back here fighting the cold when you're at the University of Florida." He hesitated, seeming to be waiting for something, and then held his hand out to Declan. "Robert Curtis. I'm in the Communications Department with Marlee."

Declan reached out his hand, but before he could speak his name, Marlee cut him off. "I'm sorry, where are my manners. Professor Curtis, this is Mr. Tate. Mr. Tate, Professor Curtis."

"Robert, please." The man shook hands with Declan.

"Declan."

Professor Curtis, easily in his early sixties, broke into the grin of a little boy meeting his hero. And perhaps he was. "I thought it was you, but for the life of me I couldn't imagine what you'd be doing on campus. And with Marlee." Marlee tried to interject, but the professor was now on a roll. "This is so exciting. I'm a huge fan, Declan, huge fan. God, that comeback against Green Bay in '08? Gutsiest thing I've ever seen."

Declan noticed Marlee's look of shock as her esteemed colleague gushed over meeting him.

"Thanks, Robert. Always great to meet someone who loves the game."

He meant it as a jab at Marlee, and from her raised eyebrow, he knew she caught it. She ignored him and turned to Robert and tried to explain what to her was the unexplainable—what she and Declan were doing together. "Mr. Tate has been kind enough to help me interject some football terms into my speech. To make it more accessible to the general public."

As if he were some kid she'd hired to give her jargon advice! He was league MVP, for Christ's sake! Declan's eyes narrowed on her at her simplistic summation, but he didn't know this guy's relationship to Marlee, and if she wanted to play it cool with him, Declan wasn't going to blow her cover. He was just about to engage the guy in deeper football talk— he knew all fans loved that—when Marlee started moving toward the door.

"It was good to see you, Robert. Have a successful semester if I don't see you when I'm in town." She was out the door with Declan trailing after her. He had barely gotten out a goodbye to the poor guy, but the professor had a smile on his face so wide that Declan didn't think he noticed.

It was a nice perk that Declan never got tired of. It never

failed to both excite and humble him. People always seemed so genuinely thrilled to meet him. Except for in Green Bay; they hated him there.

They walked to the car, Marlee a few paces in front of him, not allowing him to even their paces. That alone was quite a feat, as Declan's normal pace was nearly twice Marlee's, despite her long, beautiful legs.

"So what's his deal?"

"What do you mean?"

"Professor Curtis. You're obviously uncomfortable around him. Old boyfriend? Boss? What?"

She shook her head, looking confused that Declan would sense some kind of "thing" with Robert Curtis. "None of the above. He's a fellow professor in the my department. I've known him for years. We're not pals or anything, but we see quite a bit of each other in the offices. Nice man." She waited at the door until Declan caught up to her and opened the door of his SUV for her.

It wasn't a long walk to the driver's-side door after he placed Marlee in the vehicle, but a lot seemed to fall into place for Declan during the journey. He got a sick feeling in his stomach and hoped that he was wrong. But a nagging sensation that started in his gut told him he was right. Declan's gut never lied.

It wasn't this Curtis guy she was uncomfortable about—it was him. Or, more precisely, the thought that one of her colleagues had seen her with him. She had obviously been trying to not introduce them, but the professor had taken matters into his own hands. And if he hadn't, Declan had been about to.

And that was also why she hadn't used his first name when she'd introduced him. *Mr. Tate.* What kind of crap was that? Nobody had ever called him Mr. Tate, not even the rookies on the team or cub reporters asking for their first interview. She was hoping the professor wouldn't know Declan by just his last name. And she'd certainly dropped their clasped hands fast enough.

Declan remembered just how much physical contact there had been between them just a short while before meeting the professor. She hadn't wanted to let go of him *then*. No, she had clung to him while she reached orgasm like he was her only safe harbor. And he'd thought that just maybe he was.

The thought of Marlee being embarrassed by her relationship with him made him ache with sadness. He thought his temper would start to rage, but it didn't even flare up. No, it was not anger he felt. Something else. Something inside of him shifted and he felt more pain than any quarterback sack had ever brought him.

Here he was thinking he'd just made a major breakthrough with Marlee, and now he felt like they were back at the beginning. Worse than that, because at the beginning Declan hadn't been in love with Marlee, and he was now.

She didn't want to be seen with him.

A door seemed to shut somewhere as Declan drove them home. No, he had to stop thinking of it like that. It wasn't his home. It was Marlee's home. He was just a short-term guest.

Chapter 16

Something was wrong with Declan. He'd been so sweet and tender in the studio and now he was barely speaking to her. They had both showered (separately, even though Marlee sexily hinted that it might save time to shower together), and were now downstairs preparing the meal.

Declan was dressed in khakis and a green linen shirt that matched the green of his eyes. Marlee had put on some knit pants and a cream sweater set. The couple of times Marlee had started a conversation he'd shut her down with one-word answers, so she'd finally given up.

He had sensed her unease when she introduced him to Robert, but he had interpreted it as something between herself and Robert, wondering if he were her boss or an old flame. She was content to let him think that what he sensed had to do with her and Robert, not her and Declan. After all, how could she make him understand something she was incapable of understanding herself?

It had been an involuntary reflex; pulling her hand away from Declan's when she saw Robert coming toward them. She had covered it well, and didn't think Declan had even realized what she'd done.

And she knew why she'd done it.

When she'd been with Justin she'd been proud to show him off to her colleagues. Her. Someone who didn't even follow baseball. But she thought she was with Justin for the long haul, thought they would marry.

And beyond her devastation to find out he was cheating on her—regularly—she knew that her fellow staff members knew why they'd broken up. Maybe they'd even known Justin was a famous playboy. It might even have been a well-meaning colleague that had sent Marlee the link about Justin.

Their breakup had made the gossip sites, too, even though Marlee had tried to stay away from Justin's public life.

On some level, she didn't want her colleagues to know she was seeing another pro ball player. Like maybe she was some groupie or something.

Or open herself up to another link sent to her with all of Declan's sexual exploits. Especially since this thing with Declan was only supposed to be for a week. She really didn't want to explain that to any of her coworkers.

She knew it was unfair to paint Declan with the brush of Justin Jones. And although she'd grown to think of Declan as someone she could be happy with, have a future with, their clock was ticking.

Declan had said himself their first night in this very kitchen that he wanted to settle down *in a couple of years*, when he had his future solidified. The more she got to know him, the less she thought he'd be happy in broadcasting. He didn't mind being the center of attention when it was on the playing field, but she didn't think Declan was really the type to seek out the limelight that would come with a career in the entertainment industry, even if it was sports related.

So, even though he may not yet realize it, it may take him more than a couple of years to be at a place in his career where he felt able to focus on home and family. Realistically, Marlee didn't want to wait that long for the possibility that she and Declan could have a future together.

Back to square one, she lamented. A week of mind-blowing sex with Declan Tate. She should have been happy with just that. And she would have been had she not gotten a glimpse of what everyday life—cooking together in the kitchen, grocery shopping, lying in bed talking after exhausting lovemaking—with Declan could be.

They moved around the kitchen in shared silence, each doing separate tasks to get the dinner prepared, Marlee lost in her thoughts of a future without Declan.

DECLAN WAS STILL PISSED ABOUT THE HAND-DROPPING incident. *Mr. Tate? Christ!* What was he, her father?

What had been despair and hurt was now working its way into a full-blown snit. There were a million women out there who would give their silicone-injected breasts away to introduce him to someone as the guy they were sleeping with. Probably more than a million—the NFL was being broadcast in Asia and Europe now.

But would any of those women want to spend a Friday night making vegetarian lasagna with him for family? Or would they want to be seen on his arm out of the spotlight? In a few years when he'd be yesterday's news?

And would any of those women make him feel as complete and peaceful as being with Marlee did?

Just what was it? It was like she didn't trust them as a couple, which didn't make sense to him. She had trusted him enough to agree to videotaping themselves. They were so good together, and not just in bed, though making love with Marlee was incredible. Declan knew it was special, that he'd never find a partner like Marlee again. Partner. Yeah—that was how he'd come to think of her, as a partner. His partner.

As if reading his mind, she handed him the strainer full of cooked lasagna noodles just as he was ready for them. Like a surgical nurse knowing every movement of the surgeon, anticipating his every need before he asked. That was the kind of pattern and rhythm he and Marlee had created. It seemed so natural and unforced because it was exactly that. Natural.

Damn her for not seeing it too. It couldn't possibly have been so comfortable so fast with anyone she'd ever been involved with before. Could it? Declan assumed not, because this feeling was so new to him. He knew damn well that no guy who smoked a pipe and wore a fedora had ever done the things with her in bed that she and Declan had done.

He finished the lasagna and put it in the oven along with the first batch of cookies. It was a tight fit, but Marlee had a great oven.

The exact same kind as his.

HER FAMILY LOVED DECLAN. SHE SHOULDN'T HAVE BEEN surprised—he'd sure won her over fast—but she was. She hadn't even realized they would know who he was. Her sisters hadn't followed sports growing up either, but apparently when you gained a husband you also gained football.

Her brothers-in-law were momentarily stunned when she introduced Declan to them all, but they regained their composure quickly and proceeded to maintain some level of dignity as they conversed with him.

Her sisters were trying their hardest to get Marlee alone in the kitchen to get the scoop on why Declan Tate was in her living room and seemed very much at home there. Due to Declan being co-chef, he was in and out of the kitchen as well, and Marlee was only able to relate her meeting Declan and their subsequent cohabitation in bits and pieces. She figured that was just as well. She didn't want to deal with any disapproval on their parts. Or warning her of her past mistake with Justin. Though it looked like anything but disapproval on her sisters' faces as they practically devoured Declan with their eyes.

No, it looked like appreciation. She certainly could understand that; she had a fine appreciation for the man herself.

Her poor nephew was awe-struck, and in some weird twist of fate, was wearing his Boston Pumas jersey with Declan's name and number on the back. Marlee hadn't even realized he was a fan, but again, football was not a subject she often brought up with her nephew. The younger kids knew the name and thought it was cool that Aunt Marlee knew a Puma, but Brent was in heaven.

Declan seemed to notice Brent's inability to speak at meeting his hero, and quickly put the boy at ease. He put his arm around him and called him Hook, and when Brent didn't understand, he pointed to the picture of a three-year-old Brent on the mantel.

"God, Aunt Marlee, I've begged you to take that down. Now look what happened!"

"Whoa, whoa, that's your Aunt Marlee's favorite photograph. She pointed it out the first time I was here. It means a lot to her." He put his arm around Brent and said, in a conspiratorial, man-to-man kind of way, "You know how sentimental women can be. Cut her some slack. She's an aunt, it's her job to embarrass you. My aunt's the same way."

Brent basked in the glow of sharing something—even an

insensitive aunt—with the great Declan Tate. He seemed to grow from a gawky boy to a young man right before their eyes.

Dinner was a controlled chaos, as it was bound to be when you had five children and six adults all enjoying good food and even better conversation. Declan asked all the adults about their work.

Marlee was again amazed at how much he remembered from what she'd told him about her family. Larry and Charlie kept trying to steer the conversation back to Declan and would ask him about certain plays he made in games they remembered. Declan would always answer their questions, but would then ask one of his own about the kids or careers of the others.

What had she expected? For Declan to sit back and hold court all through dinner about the time he threw a seventy yard pass…yada, yada, yada?

That was exactly what Justin had done.

Not that her family would have minded, but equal speaking time was had by all the adults. Declan saw to that.

As the meal wound down, the kids excused themselves and then all but Brent went into Marlee's den, where they knew she had a well-watched collection of children's movies.

It was the first time Marlee could remember Brent staying at the table after the other kids had gone to watch a movie. He couldn't take his eyes off Declan, sat by him at dinner, hung on every word he said.

She knew how he felt.

Declan and she began to clear plates, but Brent put his arm on Declan's to stop him. "It's okay, Declan, I'll help Aunt Marlee." There was a sudden silence as all the adults, especially Brent's parents Susan and Charlie, sat stunned. Declan thanked Brent and allowed the boy to help Marlee clear the table, joining his aunt in the kitchen.

As soon as Marlee and Brent had left the living room and were out of earshot, Marlee's oldest sister, Susan, spoke up. "Okay. First of all, thank you. It's like pulling teeth to get that kid to do anything around the house, and even if it's only to impress you, the fact that he volunteered to help out…well…I'd like to say I'm speechless, but of course I never am." The others knowingly laughed as Susan continued, "Second of all…"

"Watch out, Declan."

"Here she goes."

"I'm surprised she's kept her mouth shut this long."

This came good-naturedly from Larry, Linda, and Charlie simultaneously, and instantly Declan had the lay of the family dynamic land. Susan was the leader. And apparently she called them as she saw them.

"I'm not going to be as antiquated as to say what are your intentions toward our sister. But what exactly are your intentions toward our sister?" She had a smile on her face, was teasing Declan, but he knew there was a real concern. He was glad, in a way. It meant that Marlee's family cared about her, cared what happened to her, cared about her future. So did Declan. Like he did in a game situation, he made a split-second decision to put his cards on the table. After all, if all went as he hoped, these people would be in his life, may even be family.

He turned around to make sure the kitchen door was closed, that Marlee and Brent were still out of earshot. He looked each of them dead in the eye and let out a big sigh and came clean. "We met Sunday. Instant attraction. We're both in town for short times, so we thought, hey, what the hell, let's see all we can of each other while we can." He let this sink in, waiting for their reaction. It was shock on their faces, all right, but Declan sensed that it was more from him being so honest with them then the fact that their younger sister had entered into an affair with a man she'd just met.

In for a penny, he thought, and continued, "But, in the midst of one of the best weeks of my life—and believe me, I've had some pretty good weeks…" He said this in a wink-wink conspiratorial tone aimed at Larry and Charlie, who nodded and smiled, apparently only able to dream of the great times Declan Tate had had in his life. The wins, the glory, the women.

They gave him a knowing look as he went on. "I began to see how much in common Marlee and I have. We have very similar upbringings, our goals for family are the same, we're both at a point in our lives where we want to settle down, get married, have kids." He stopped there at the questioning looks the two couples were giving each other, and realized that maybe he'd let the cat out of Marlee's bag.

She hadn't told them she wanted to start a family? But she'd told *him*? The thought gave Declan a tingling feeling, and he decided to look upon that fact as a positive sign. "We even have the same tastes and styles. You wouldn't believe how similar our houses, and especially our kitchens, are to each other." This got more looks, as they all knew the importance of Marlee's kitchen to her.

"Bottom line…I'm in love with your sister."

He waited for a reaction, but it was delayed as the two couples could only stare at him. Linda was the one who regained her composure first. "That's wonderful, Declan. Really." The others quickly joined in with congratulations, and Charlie, sitting next to him, even gave Declan a playful slug to the upper arm.

Susan continued, "I'm sorry to seem so shocked. We're

happy for you, truly. It's just…I don't think any of us would ever have seen Marlee with a football player."

Declan started to say that even Marlee couldn't see Marlee with a football player, but Linda spoke first. "I mean, after the whole Justin Jones thing? I'm kind of shocked she even gave you the time of day."

Declan felt a stab of pain, similar to the one he felt after the Robert Curtis incident. No. Much, much deeper. Who the fuck was Justin Jones? Wait. "Justin Jones the Red Sox shortstop?"

He knew his strangled voice gave away the fact that Marlee hadn't told him about—*fuck!*—her relationship with the All-Star shortstop.

"Oh, great, Linda. You totally blew that," Susan said to her sister, giving her the evil eye.

"No, it's okay," he said, trying to cover. "We decided not to do all the exes talk." So not true, though they hadn't exactly divulged all of their past lovers to each other. And yet she'd told him all about her college boyfriend and a couple of other short-term relationships.

Never one mention of Justin Jones.

The two couples exchanged looks amongst themselves, and Declan tried to get the focus off Linda's blunder. Though it was all *he* could think about.

"Besides, I said I was in love with Marlee. I didn't say she loved me back."

Charlie seemed flummoxed. "But…but…how could she *not* love you?"

Declan chuckled as Charlie became embarrassed over his outburst. "Thanks for the vote of confidence, Charlie. Too bad it wasn't you I fell in love with." They all laughed loudly at that one as Marlee and Brent came back to collect more dishes.

"What'd I miss? It sounds hilarious." She had seemed

pleased all evening that her family had all taken to Declan as they had.

"Oh, I was just telling Charlie here about one party we had in Cleveland that got a little wild," Declan lied. The others nodded with him, taking him into the fold by covering for him. And for Linda.

Marlee put on her disapproving professor face and said, "Oh. Come on, Brent." She herded the reluctant teenager back into the kitchen with another load.

The thought that Brent was missing stories of his hero and parties, possibly with naked women, took the do-gooder spirit right out of the kid, and he made his second trip into the kitchen with a scowl on his face.

"Great, now he's going to be begging me to tell him that story," Charlie said, laughing. Susan gave him an understanding look. Raising a fifteen-year-old in today's world couldn't be easy.

"Sorry. I just love getting a rise out of Marlee. Did you see the look she shot me?" Declan said.

"Oh yeah, we know that look—don't we, Charlie?" Larry said, as Linda elbowed him but smiled. "The Reeves girls sure can turn on the disparaging looks when they want to."

"Hey, don't knock that look—it's imperative to raising your children, buster."

Declan enjoyed the camaraderie. It reminded him of his family dinners in Ohio. Marlee would fit in there as easily as Declan fit in with her family.

Would that ever happen?

As if reading his mind, Susan got them back to the subject at hand. "So what's the game plan, Declan? With Marlee, I mean."

They were all ears, but Declan didn't know what to say. "Susan, I can honestly say it's the first time in my life that I've walked to the huddle and had absolutely no idea what play to call."

The men nodded their heads knowingly, while the women just looked at each other, hoping for a nugget of advice to give Declan. None came.

Was it because Marlee still loved Justin Jones?

MARLEE AND BRENT MADE ANOTHER TRIP AND THEN Declan joined them in the kitchen to make some lattes to go with the cookies. He loaded a tray with a plate of cookies and glasses of milk and, after getting Marlee's permission for the kids to eat their dessert in the den while they watched their movie, took it in to them. Brent went with him. Marlee didn't know if it was Declan or the cookies he was following, figuring both were a draw for Brent.

She brought the lattes and cookies out for the adults, who hadn't moved from the table, comfortable with each other, comfortable with their conversations. Declan hadn't come back from the den yet, and she went to retrieve him before his drink turned cold. She stopped in the doorway, not wanting to disturb the scene in front of her.

Declan was seated on her old couch with Grace in his lap and Heather beside him. Graham was on his other side and Matt sat on the floor at his feet. Brent was in the leather recliner to their right. She leaned against the doorjamb and watched the kids that were so dear to her heart. And Declan. They all had their backs to Marlee and she was able to watch them without their noticing.

They had pulled the coffee table up to Declan's legs, Matt using it as a desk for his cookies and the rest of them periodically leaning over to dip their cookie in their respective glasses of milk. *Despicable Me* was playing and they all sat in rapt attention, even Brent and Declan. Grace had her arm around Declan's neck and her head rested on his shoulder. Heather was cuddled in close and Graham was sitting cross-legged with his right knee overlapping Declan's thigh.

Grace had a sniffle and she not-so-daintily wiped her nose on Declan's shirt. Marlee could see that Declan had noticed; his shoulder rose a little. He rubbed Grace's back and brushed her hair away from her little forehead, and with just that motion, Marlee realized she was head over heels in love with Declan Tate.

It hit her like a ton of bricks. Though she really shouldn't be surprised. It had all been leading to this. The emotions she had for Declan. The incredible lovemaking they had today. Seeing him with her family.

She knew. She loved Declan.

She had thought she was in love with Justin two years ago, and perhaps she was. But it wasn't this. It wasn't this deep feeling, this contentment she felt just watching Declan. There was trust here.

There was no way she would have made those tapes if there wasn't.

She was interrupted from her epiphany by Linda's gentle voice behind her. "He'll make a wonderful father. Someday." The last word was said more softly, as if it didn't have to belong to the thought if Marlee didn't want it to.

Unconsciously, Marlee's hand stroked her abdomen as she thought about Declan and fatherhood. Her nieces and nephews clung to Declan like they had known him their whole lives. Declan definitely had the touch. And yes, he would make a great father, whether his children were boys or girls, interested in sports or Disney movies.

But it was Linda's "someday" that stuck in Marlee's ear.

Declan still had a someday, whereas Marlee wanted to start a family soon. She was still young, but wanted at least two, maybe three kids. And just spending time with her nieces and nephews wasn't enough anymore to placate her maternal yearnings.

Listening to Kathy talk about her child the other night had only driven that fact home to Marlee.

As the evening came to an end, they saw her family out and then cleaned up the kitchen in a silence similar to the one they had shared when preparing the dinner. Declan had continued to seem distant. He wasn't short with her or mad. When she asked a question, he answered her, when she made a joke, he laughed, but Marlee was doing all the work.

Growing weary of holding up both ends, she announced she was going to bed as soon as the kitchen was back to its original spotlessness. Thinking Declan would be right behind her, she was surprised to hear him say he'd be up in a while. As she stared at him with shock, bordering on hurt, he came to her and placed a sweet kiss on her forehead, turned her toward the stairs, and swatted her bottom. "Go on. I want to use your computer in the den and make a copy of one of my tapes. I won't be that long."

She gave him a questioning look, which he read in an instant.

"Not a copy of *that* tape. I told you you'd have the only copy. I'd love to make a copy for myself, but only if you want me to."

Relieved, and not surprised that he was being true to his word, she went to bed without him.

It was her intention to stay awake until Declan joined her. They only had two more nights together and she didn't plan to spend them sleeping. She left the bedside lamp on Declan's side turned on. Her good intentions were for naught, as the busy activity of the day, not to mention the draining sex in the studio, caused her to quickly fall asleep.

She hadn't had time to fall into a deep sleep, so she wasn't sure if she were waking or dreaming as she felt her body turn to her back and felt hard hands on her hips. When those same hands pushed up the filmy nightgown she was wearing to her neck and wet, hungry lips clamped down on her breast and began to suck her hard, she knew it was no dream.

She moaned and writhed beneath Declan, her body rapidly catching up to his in arousal. This man could have her from heavy sleep to dripping wet in under four seconds. She brought her hands up to touch his face, and it seemed as though that act of intimacy was too much for him. He grabbed both of her hands in one of his and pinned them to the pillow above her head. At the same moment his other hand slid into her, measured her wetness, and, deeming her ready, he guided his sheathed, hard penis to her.

"Look at me, Marlee. See my face as I ram into you."

It was not the gentle tone he had used this afternoon. It was the sexy voice he had used all week with her. It worked.

She gasped and raised her hips to meet his rough entrance. She clenched her muscles around him as she wrapped her thighs around his hips. His eyes held hers, and the look he gave her was fierce and deep. He held her hands and relentlessly drove into her. The tenderness gone. The gentleness gone. Left was a primitive, possessive mating that had them both crying out with their release within minutes.

Chapter 17

When she woke up the next morning, Marlee reached for Declan but found his side of the bed empty. It was funny how easily she thought of it as "his" side of the bed. She ran her hand down the cool sheets and realized he must have been out of bed for quite some time. All the heat from his body had gone. And the man could generate some heat.

She threw on a robe and went downstairs to the kitchen. The coffee pot was nearly full and there was a note placed in front of it with her mug sitting as a paperweight. It said he was running some errands and would be back in the afternoon.

Marlee tried not to let the note get her down. Of course he had to run some errands. He was leaving tomorrow for a week, and he had been spending every waking moment with her. He probably had a million things to do.

A nagging feeling crept up. She couldn't quite put a name to it. Sort of like....dread? It was natural enough, she supposed, to be dreading parting with Declan. She had become very attached to the sex they were having. The all-out, rough-and-tumble sex that she had never experienced before, and feared she never would again.

Liar. It isn't just the sex you've become attached to and you know it. And besides, the best sex you had with Declan all week was yesterday, when it wasn't rough and tumble, when it was... making love.

The thought wasn't as scary now that she'd admitted she loved Declan, if only to herself. In bed last night, she had hoped for a repeat of the slow, sensual lovemaking they had shared earlier at the studio. She felt closer to Declan that way. Thought that maybe she'd even be able to voice her feelings to him. But the cataclysmic mating that Declan initiated, though wonderful, allowed no room for proclamations of love. And maybe that was just what he'd planned.

Maybe he sensed her feelings. She certainly hadn't masked them at the studio.

Of course. It all made sense. It was shortly after that when Declan started acting weird. First the thing with Professor Curtis, then the silence before and after her family had arrived. The slam-bam sex. And then rushing out of here this morning before she woke up.

He had figured out she loved him and was trying to get through the next two days without her confessing the news to him. He didn't want to embarrass her when she blurted out she loved him and he could only say..."Uh, thanks."

That was so Declan, wanting to spare her feelings. No wonder she loved him.

Marlee's heart ached for what couldn't be, but she wanted to let Declan off the hook. She cared for him that much. She would act as if nothing happened, be as light and carefree about Declan and her as she'd been earlier in the week. That would make it easier for him. He wouldn't have to avoid her for the next twenty-four hours. She could hold it together that long.

Then she would start her tour and would be alone in a hotel room far from home. The perfect setting to feel sorry for herself and mourn a broken heart. And probably watch the video file of them together about a zillion times.

After the tour she'd come home and get serious about her search for suitable men. Look how quickly she fell for Declan, and he was totally unsuitable. If she met the love of her life when she got off the tour in March, there was no telling how quickly things could move from there.

The thought did nothing to cheer up Marlee. A voice in the back of her head screamed, *You can't meet the love of your life in March...you've already met him.* She tried to silence the voice, but couldn't. Probably because it was right.

Her heart became heavy all over again.

DECLAN CAME HOME AROUND THREE AND THEY DECIDED to order Chinese delivery later for dinner. Neither felt like cooking. That in and of itself should have been a red flag to them both, but they chalked it up to being tired, and wanting to pack and seeing to other odds and ends.

Marlee dashed out to do a few errands of her own. Pick up dry cleaning, pick up messages, and correspondence from her office. She invited Declan to join her, but he asked if he could do some laundry and Marlee showed him where the detergent and things were. She offered to do it for him later, but he mumbled something about having to do things for himself and she left him to it.

It was all very civilized, very polite, and only slightly strained.

It took Marlee longer than she thought at her office, so she decided to get the Chinese on her way home. She called Declan to ask what he'd like and to tell him about this wonderful vegetarian sweet and sour tofu that the Golden Panda did. He agreed that the tofu sounded great.

Though the conversation was not as free and easy as it had been all week, it flowed while they ate their food. Marlee was determined not to say anything that Declan may construe as clingy or emotional.

As they were clearing away their dishes, she finally wound up her courage and said, "What's wrong, Declan?"

A look of pain crossed his face, and then it turned to something she couldn't quite name. Was that pity? Was he feeling sorry for her?

Oh, crap. She shouldn't have asked the question. She really didn't want to have "the talk" on their last night together. What would be the point, anyway?

"Never mind. Forget I asked. Here." She held her hand out to him. "Come with me."

She knew she wanted to watch their sex tape with him. But as she entered the room and saw the flash drive with the red X sitting next to her computer, another idea struck her.

She couldn't seem to tell Declan she was in love with him. Did not want to put her heart in his hands when he'd said he couldn't count on a future until he had his next career figured out. Justin had humiliated her too badly for her to be able to put herself out there like that. But she could let Declan know how much this week had meant to her in a different way.

She moved to the desk, still holding his hand. Sitting at her desk chair, she reluctantly let go of his hand to put the flash drive in the USB port of her laptop.

"Are we going to watch this?" Declan said from where he came to stand behind her chair. He placed his hands on her shoulders and squeezed.

"In a minute. I just want to do this first." She copied the file to her laptop, then ejected the flash drive and grabbed an identical one from her pile of empty drives and plugged it into the laptop. She copied it over to the new drive and then ejected it. She moved the file that had been on her laptop to the trash and deleted it. She used this laptop too much at work and when she traveled to risk opening that file by mistake when anyone was in her presence.

Swiveling in the chair, she held the new drive out to Declan. "I want you to have this copy. I completely trust you with it."

It wasn't the declaration of love she wanted to profess, but in some ways, it was just as important. Declan had no way of knowing how hard this was for her, how much it took to give him a copy of it.

"Marlee," he said softly. Almost so softly that she didn't hear him. "Are you sure?" he asked.

She nodded. "Yes. It only seems fair that you hold one too. I could be a crazy stalker fan whose whole goal this week was to get you having sex on tape and then sell it to the tabloids."

His laughter was deep and rich and she smiled up at him. He leaned down and kissed the top of her head. "You sure played me, then."

It felt good to banter with him again, the tension of today drifting away. He nodded to her large TV. "Do you have a hook up to stream from your laptop to the TV?" She nodded, feeling a little nervous about the upcoming featured attraction. But this was truly a now-or-never situation if she wanted to view it with Declan.

She put her drive back into the USB port while Declan slid his into the front pocket of his jeans. She clicked a few things to get the streaming set up and then she appeared on the TV screen—looking at Declan as he walked toward where she leaned against the desk in the studio.

"Come on," he said from behind her. She rose from her chair and he took her hand, leading her to the leather recliner and, after seating himself, settling Marlee upon his lap.

He put the footstool of the recliner out and put the back down just a little so he could slide Marlee from his lap to the vee of his spread thighs, her bottom cradled by his crotch, his long thighs on the outside of hers. He pulled her taut body to him so her back lay upon his chest. She had changed into sweats and a long-sleeve T-shirt when she got home, and the material was soft and clingy against her quickly heating skin.

She lay back and watched the tape. It was moving quickly, just as Marlee and Declan had that first time on the desk. When the Marlee on screen told Declan she wanted him to take her hard and fast, the Marlee in Declan's arms gasped and flung her hands to her face as if to cover her embarrassment.

Declan instantly began to stroke her neck and back, and his arm reached around to pull her hands from her face. She was reluctant, but he persisted.

"Don't be embarrassed, baby. It was wonderful. You made me so hard when you said that. Look at my face there. God, I'm ready to eat you up."

She raised her eyes to look at the TV again. Sure enough, Declan looked like a man possessed. It gave her a tiny rush to see what she did to him, and her body relaxed. Declan felt it and tried to get her more comfortable. "You know, you lied to me, Marlee."

As she turned her head to his face to see what he meant, he gently took the back of her neck and pressed her head forward again.

"Just watch, I'll talk. You like it when I talk during sex." He gave her a tiny squeeze. "Yep, you lied to me about your sisters. You said they were much prettier than you. Now, I could accuse you of being coy and fishing for compliments, but you wouldn't even know how to go about doing that, would you, professor?"

Marlee shook her head, her hair brushing along the bottom of Declan's chin. On screen, Declan had gotten Marlee's jeans off by now and was putting on a condom, readying to take Marlee as she lay across the desk, her arms outstretched for Declan.

"No, I didn't think that was your style. So, I came to the conclusion that you have no idea how beautiful you are. How sexy, how hot you can be. Look at that, Marlee. Look at your face as I enter you, God, there isn't a woman alive more beautiful than you right there."

She knew he could hear her swallow. It was more of a gulp, and it brought her head back with a force that almost banged Declan's chin. In his arms, all the tension in her body released and it was if she had turned from steel to jelly in an instant. He cuddled her closer and dipped his head so he could nuzzle her neck and be right at her ear as he whispered to her.

"You see, it didn't take me long once I was inside you, Marlee. I probably shouldn't admit to that…" They both let out a low chuckle. "But it's like that with you, Marlee. As soon as I'm inside you and I feel you pulling on me, wanting me, clenching around me…I'm lost. You do that to me." On the TV, Declan reached his climax, lifting his head, almost in agony, shuddering deeply and calling Marlee's name.

She had been there, had been beneath him as he'd climaxed, seen him do it, yet watching the effect she had on him left her in awe. Seeing Declan drive into her in front of her while hearing his sexy whispers and feeling his muscled chest behind her was making Marlee's head spin. It was also making her very aroused. It was a natural instinct to want to burrow herself into Declan.

She wiggled her fanny, scooched herself up so she was tight against him and wasn't surprised to feel his erection, already hard and long, against her.

His arms that had been wrapped around her upper arms, afraid she would bolt, loosened. One dropped to her tummy and began a light, feathery, circular motion. The other hand swooped her hair off her neck and to one side of her head, freeing her neck for his mouth. His hand then landed on her upper thigh. It seemed to burn through the light cotton of her sweatpants.

Marlee began to rub her bottom against Declan. His lips nibbled on her neck, with tenderness, not his usual ferocity. They continued to watch the screen, transfixed by the images in front of them.

On the TV, they were cleaning themselves up now. Collecting clothes, giving each other sly glances, Marlee even giggling. Declan turned down the volume of the TV completely, with only his voice to invade Marlee's senses.

"God, I love when I can make you giggle. I love all the sounds I get from you."

Marlee let out a soft moan of agreement. She watched as Sex Tape Declan made his way to the camera as Marlee finished righting her sweater. He had his eye on that sweater all day, she recalled.

The screen went blank and Marlee started to move, but Declan stilled her. "Wait."

She started to turn in his arms, but Declan's movements made her stop. He took the hand from her tummy and put it under her shirt, against her trembling skin. He held his hand there, not moving it, as if to hold in place. There was a small gap of space and then the TV filled with the scene from yesterday, when they were on the chairs. The arousal Marlee had felt just a moment ago watching them have fast and furious sex on the desk paled in comparison with what she felt as she watched her give herself to the man she loved.

Nearly mimicking the action on the TV, Declan's hands were everywhere on her now, but still so slowly. One hand was cradling a breast over the satin cups of her bra, kneading her sensitive skin, feeling the nipple become rigid, rolling it between his thumb and forefinger. The other hand slid in her sweatpants, past her panties to find her already swollen and throbbing.

"You see why I wanted us to make this tape? I can feel how wet it makes you to watch us, Marlee." He slipped a finger inside her and there was no doubt that his words were true. Her passage was slick and hot with her juices. Her breath caught and she ground herself against his jeans.

They continued to watch the tape as Declan made love to Marlee with his fingers. She reached behind her and, after some fumbling, freed Declan's pulsing erection from his jeans. In an instant she was stroking him, clasping him hard, her hands behind her back to reach him, which only pushed her breasts out more for his hand.

"Look at your face, Marlee. See what we do to each other." He hesitated, seemed to debate how far to go. "See what *I* do to you. Watch how hard you come for me, Marlee. For *me*."

She was so close, both in his arms and on the TV. He lifted the fingers inside of her and brushed his thumb hard across her swollen nub. "Watch yourself come apart as you come in my arms. Watch it, Marlee. Feel it. Feel me. Me, making you come. Only me, Marlee. Only me."

As if she were synchronized with her onscreen self, Marlee threw her head back and her whole body convulsed as her orgasm tore through her. Declan's fingers never stilled, making her rise again almost immediately. "See, Marlee. Look at your face. See how hard you come, like you are right now. It's so good, baby. It nearly makes me spill, myself, just watching you get there."

Her mind was slowly coming back into focus. Declan's throbbing penis was still in her grasp but she had stopped stroking, her attention riveted to the TV. On the tape she and Declan had been flammable in the deep chair—you could see the vulnerability on each of their faces, but that was nothing new; they had been looking into each other's eyes the whole time. There was nothing to hide.

She was just about to turn herself around and take Declan in her mouth when something on the screen stopped her.

Declan was walking to the camera, just like he had after their earlier coupling. This time, because they were at the talk-show set, the camera was angled differently, and not only could you see Declan walking toward the camera, you could see Marlee behind him. She was watching Declan move with a look of a love in her eyes that was obvious to read. Declan, having had his back to her as he'd gone to the camera, hadn't seen that look. He'd never seen that look in Marlee's eyes.

It was hunger and passion and appreciation and—undoubtedly—love.

The love, the vulnerability, was written all over her face, plain for all to see. Plain for Declan to see. She heard him gasp and tighten behind her. She could only imagine what he was feeling. Here was a man who had just videotaped himself and his week-long fling having sex, and here she was all moony-eyed behind him, shooting looks of love at his back, as if she were Cupid and could pierce his heart.

She was humiliated and embarrassed and she hoped that if she turned and put her mouth on Declan that he'd forget what he'd just seen.

As she tried to turn, he held her in place, and whispered in her ear, "Did you ever look at Justin Jones like that?"

MARLEE'S BODY FROZE IN HIS ARMS AND DECLAN instantly knew he'd fucked up.

She released his hard cock, which slightly deflated at the loss of contact. She scooted forward, then turned around to face him.

"Just what do you know about me and Justin?"

"Nothing from you, that's for sure. But I spent some time in here last night googling the shit out of the both of you. Pretty interesting reading."

It had crushed him, seeing the photos of a happy Marlee with Jones's arm wrapped around her. It had been two years ago and seemed to have lasted several months. There were some old gossip site entries about their breakup due to Jones's womanizing.

"If you saw anything about us at all online then you know that he was unfaithful to me. That he broke my trust, over and over."

"And you're punishing me for his sins. You do know that all professional athletes don't cheat on their partner, right?"

"Of course I do."

She was so close, her face just a movement away from his. He should just stop right now and kiss her. But he couldn't. The week of trying to prove to her that they had so much in common had been a lost cause from the beginning.

Because some fucker that also happened to be a professional athlete had broken her trust and then broken her heart.

"Joey and Kathy. You think he's out cheating on her?" he

asked, though he wasn't sure what point he was trying to make.

"No, of course not."

"I know a ton of players that are completely faithful to their wives or girlfriends. We're not all Justin Jones, you know."

"I know," she said quietly. And with not a lot of conviction.

"Are you still in love with him?"

She reared back like he'd hit her. "What? No. Why would you even think that?"

"Because you didn't mention him."

"Did *you* share every relationship with me?"

"The important ones, yeah."

"That's why the aggressive behavior in bed last night, wasn't it? It was after you'd been online. You were...what? Trying to stake your claim?"

"Are you saying he still has some kind of hold on you? Some sort of claim?"

"What? Of course not. Don't be ridiculous."

"So why didn't you ever mention him?"

She stood now, stepped away from the chair. "Are you kidding me?"

Her clothes were in disarray from where his hands had been on her. Even furious, she was still sexy as hell. It didn't help that his cock noticed it too and hardened once again.

Looking down at him, she easily noticed his growing cock, and threw her hands up as if in dismay. "Unbelievable. This gets you hard. Well, I guess I really shouldn't have expected adult behavior from someone who plays a game for a living!"

For Declan, it was the final nail, and the lid of his relationship with Marlee closed on the coffin. He rose out of the chair, zipped up, and started to walk from the room. At the doorway he turned back. He knew she heard him stop, but she didn't turn to face him, just kept staring at the screen of her laptop.

"I tried to make you see, Marlee—all week long I tried. But you refuse to see. Refuse to see, or refuse to let go of your image of pro athletes because of Justin fucking Jones. Either way....it's both our losses." She didn't turn around, but Declan knew she heard every word.

He slept in the guest room that night. He'd wanted to go to a hotel, but that would have meant going into Marlee's room to pack up his stuff, and she had barricaded herself in there. He'd gone to the kitchen from the den to cool off for a moment. He was going to go back and try to talk to her about it. Get her to open up about being hurt by Justin Jones, and what that did to her perception of Declan. But when he went back, she wasn't in the den, but her bedroom door was closed, and that pissed him off all over again. Declan didn't want to give her the satisfaction of knocking on the door, begging to be let in, even if was only to pack his bags and leave. No, let her stew in there, wondering what he was doing.

He was doing nothing but cursing himself for being a fool. First for torturing himself with the pictures online of Justin and Marlee together. What had he been thinking? And secondly for even bringing it up to Marlee. If she didn't want him knowing about her relationship with the ball player, then he should have just left it the hell alone.

Well, ultimately, he'd ended up at the same place he was before, with her unwilling to see beyond this week and him trying to get her to see past it.

He felt exhausted, as if he'd spent all week running in circles.

In a way, he guessed he had.

MARLEE SPENT THE NIGHT IN AGONY. SHE WAITED FOR Declan to come into the bedroom. Even if he was leaving early, he needed to come in here to get his stuff. She could hear him downstairs and then in the guest room, and she figured that was where he was spending the night. Part of her was relieved and part was in despair.

She really wasn't that upset about him bringing up Justin. No, it was the look of raw devotion that had shone on her face, unbeknownst to Declan, that had set her off. She didn't want him to know that, of course. She was mortified that he'd even seen it. She couldn't make it worse by drawing attention to it. So she had worked herself into a justified snit about his perceived jealousy over Justin.

She huddled under the covers, still in her clothes, wishing Declan was with her.

Chapter 18

"Aaaannnddd cut. Great, Declan, that was just great. I think that's all we need...that one's a keeper." The director was a recent NYU grad that the public relations firm had hired to tape all their clients' audition tapes. He was young and arty with a goatee and an earring, but Declan had come to like him in the three days they had worked together. He had some good tips for Declan and had really put him at ease, allowing him to get some good stuff on tape.

The kid handed a flash drive to Declan. It was a customized drive with a crazy design that Declan had seen the kid use on his business cards and was stenciled on his bag. Must be his insignia or trademark or something quirky that Declan didn't get. Artists. And they said jocks were weird.

Well, maybe only Marlee said that.

The thought of Marlee hit him like a nose tackle with an axe to grind, just as it had every time he'd thought of her since Sunday. Oh, they'd been polite enough his last morning, leaving each other alone in Marlee's room to each pack their things one at a time, even muddling around the kitchen getting coffee. But it was tense, and there was no mention of the tape, and no mention of them seeing each other again.

Damn. He was so close. He knew she hadn't been pissed about him bringing up Justin, not really. Not until the end. Something had turned, and damned if he could figure it out. Maybe that was the problem—he thought he could figure Marlee out. *No fucking way.*

He took the flash drive from the director. "Thanks for all your work, Rowdy. I feel pretty good about the tape. I just want to take it back to the hotel and watch it again, maybe compare it to the ones I made last week in Boston, see if I've improved."

"Well, whatever you did there last week worked, because you were ready on Monday. It was just nice we had some time to polish a few things. Okay, well, your agent has made arrangements for a courier to pick up the drive from your hotel this afternoon. It'll go to a tech place that will burn DVDs and then deliver them to ABC, CBS, NBC, FOX, and ESPN by three so they have time to look at them. It's my understanding that your agent has you booked back to back tomorrow and Friday with them all, right?"

"Yep. I meet with the first one at ten tomorrow morning, then a late lunch with another, the same on Friday with the other two, then I go to Connecticut late Friday to meet with ESPN."

"Well, the tape's ready, Declan, so it's up to you now."

"Thanks again, Rowdy, it was a pleasure working with you."

"You too. Now that we're done and I don't have to direct you anymore, I don't mind telling you that you're my hero. I've thought you were the greatest for years. I was so thrilled when I found out I was going to work with you." The kid's face lit up as he spoke.

Declan smiled and thanked the kid, thanked the entire crew, and went back to his hotel, shaking his head in amusement and frustration.

See, Marlee, everybody loves football players. Even artists. Everyone but you.

Back at the hotel, Declan put the flash drive on the desk so he wouldn't have to root around for it when the courier came. He went over to his suitcase to find the three flash drives he'd brought with him. The ones he'd made with Marlee. He pulled out four of the flash drive cartridges. That was weird. He could have sworn he'd only packed three. He'd only made three. He carried them all to the desk so he could sort them out. Three were clearly labeled "Wednesday," "Thursday," and "Friday," writing with the Sharpie he'd done right there in the studio. He picked up the fourth drive. There was no writing, but there was a large red X.

No way. Marlee had that drive.

He picked up the cartridge and turned it over, unable to believe it was the drive that Marlee had taken. There was a piece of tape on the other side, like something had been attached to it. He rummaged deeper into his bag and felt a small piece of paper. A note. From Marlee.

Declan's palms suddenly became wet and he wished he had a towel snapped to his pants like he did during games so he could wipe his hands dry. He pulled out the folded paper and opened it up.

Declan,

I'm so sorry for the way I behaved last night. And I so enjoyed our incredible week. It's unfortunate that our last night together was spent apart, but I can't thank you enough for the best week of my life.

I wanted to give you my copy of the tape so you would have both. It's just my way of saying how much I trust you. And also, I thought I'd want to watch it over and over, but now I realize that it would be too painful for me, so I want you to have it.

Marlee

P.S. I would never had made a tape with Justin Jones—I didn't trust him like I do you.

DECLAN WALKED OVER TO THE BED, THE NOTE STILL IN his hand, the drive placed on the desk next to the one from Rowdy. She signed it just plain "Marlee." Not "love, Marlee." Or "yours, Marlee."

Unbelievable. She'd given him the tape. She'd trusted him enough to give him both tapes. He let out a soft chuckle that turned into a gut-busting laugh as he thought of all the repercussions of her actions. And exactly what he'd done that Sunday morning in her room while she was making coffee.

There was a soft knock on the door and Declan went to answer it, still holding the note and laughing. It was the courier coming for the tape. Beckoning the kid in, Declan went to the dresser to get his wallet for some money to tip the kid. After all, his future was in this scrawny, pimply faced kid's hands.

"The flash drive's on the desk, there, kid. The one with the goofy markings."

Declan tipped him handsomely, sent him on his way after obliging the kid with an autograph, then went to the bed to sit down and grab his phone.

He had to call her. It was too funny, and she'd see that. The tape would be a good opener, then they could laugh about how juvenile they'd been their last day. He'd ask her forgiveness about even bringing up Justin Jones. Then Declan would press her to see him again. He'd even fly on Saturday to wherever she was.

If he remembered correctly, she was just getting to Duke today, her first lecture tomorrow, then just over to North Carolina for a Friday lecture.

Declan put the phone down. He'd call her tomorrow night, after her first lecture. He'd have met with a couple of the networks by then and that would give him something to talk to her about in case she was being icy. Either way, Declan would melt her down somehow, until she agreed to see him again.

They were not over. There was still a shot.

Feeling born again, Declan threw on his jacket and headed out of the room, in search of some food. He didn't even see the drive with Rowdy's custom label on it sitting on the desk as he walked by.

MARLEE UNPACKED HER BAGS IN HER HOTEL ROOM IN Chapel Hill. She stayed in the same room for several days while she made the stops of Duke and North Carolina, their campuses being so close. She was happy to see that her suits had made the flight without too much wrinkling. Hanging them up now would ensure that her navy one would be ready for her first lecture tomorrow night.

She'd been pleased with her meeting with the secretary of education in DC, and felt she had an ally. Now, if she knocked it out of the park (she couldn't believe she was using a baseball analogy!) at each of these universities, she could report back that the groundwork was in place for a sweeping initiative.

Even though each stop was only for one or two nights, Marlee always completely unpacked her bags, putting things in the hotel drawers. It made it feel just a little more like home. And on this trip, Marlee needed that. Home had a warmer, more heartfelt longing attached to it now. Home made her think of Declan.

The ache in her heart as she thought of Declan had almost become familiar to her. There was no cure, though Häagen-Dazs seemed to help. Until she realized that the ice cream made her think of Declan too. Maybe she should try chocolate.

With her bags unpacked, she turned to her satchel where she had her notes for the lecture and the flash drive that held her PowerPoint and the video she opened with. She hadn't needed them when she'd met with the secretary. She took them out and placed them on the table of her room, then went to put the satchel away, but was surprised by its bulk. Something was still in there. She looked inside and saw a blinding blast of yellow. Puzzled, she reached in to take it out. As soon as her hand touched the soft wool, her stomach clenched and her throat tightened.

It was Declan's scarf. He had given her his scarf.

The scent of Declan seemed to emanate from the fabric, and it pulled at Marlee. It smelled of Declan and of Marlee and of Boston and of her home. Her senses began to shift.

She pulled it fully out of the bag and went to wrap it around her but was stopped. The scarf was wrapped around something. She unwound the fabric, gently, as if what lay beneath was something fragile and breakable, just like Marlee's nerves at the moment.

As it became obvious that the object was a thumb drive, Marlee's breath caught. No, it couldn't be. She'd given their tape to Declan.

She'd decided that Sunday morning that she would need closure. Much as she delighted in the idea of being able to view Declan and herself whenever she wanted, she knew that it would only torture her. Her heart breaking now was bad enough; she didn't need to relive it whenever she became melancholy and decided to gaze upon the man she loved.

And ultimately, she trusted Declan not to post the video anywhere public. She'd never truly trusted Justin enough to even *make* a tape with him, let alone give him sole ownership of the file.

There was a note attached to the drive and she smiled at, once again, the similarities between herself and Declan. They had even used paper from the same tablet, the one on her desk at home.

Marlee,

I'm so sorry I ruined our last tonight together by bringing up your relationship with Justin. It was none of my business, and it was obvious he caused you a lot of pain. I can only hope that you don't look back on our week together and have those memories bring you any pain.

I also see what his cheating did to your trust, and what a gift it was that you made a copy of our tape for me. I would never betray that trust, but so you are never left doubting me—or us—I am giving it back to you, though it kills me to do so.

So, here is the tape, you now have both to do with as you like.

It was incredible, Marlee, I hope you know that.

Declan

MARLEE DIDN'T KNOW WHETHER TO LAUGH OR CRY, AND her body betrayed her by doing both. In some twisted O. Henry "Gift of the Magi" freaky way, she and Declan had exchanged tapes.

God, she loved that man. God, she missed him.

She read the note again, looking for any hidden meanings, but didn't find any.

God, could she ever just turn off her thoughts off, not

have to think everything to death? That had been her problem all along, hadn't it? Thinking too much, remembering Justin's betrayal, and not just trusting her feelings. Trusting that she loved Declan.

That Declan would never betray her.

Suddenly exhausted, she threw the drive back into her satchel and got out of her clothes. She let them fall to the floor and didn't make a move to hang them up. She set the alarm and climbed into bed, clutching Declan's note and wearing nothing but his scarf.

Chapter 19

What kind of perverted game are you playing with me, boy?" The burly man in a very expensive suit growled at Declan as an assistant led him into the man's office.

Not exactly the greeting Declan was expecting. This was the head of a network sports division? Declan had his hand outstretched to shake but quickly pulled it back. "Excuse me?"

"I said, what kind of sick game are you playing here?"

"I don't know what you mean."

The assistant, sensing an oncoming storm, turned and fled, closing the door and leaving Declan all alone with the executive. The office was palatial, with a majestic view of the city. It was also huge, and Declan was glad of that as it gave him some room to maneuver until he could figure out what had made Henry Albright so incensed.

They'd never met before, but had spoken on the phone when Henry wanted to personally express his interest in having Declan join his team. He had been very jovial on the phone, very ingratiating. Not at all like the man now in front of him—red in the face with rage, all seemingly aimed at Declan.

"Mr. Albright. Henry. I'm sorry, I really don't have any idea what your talking about."

"That goddamn tape of yours that's what I'm talking about." He had risen from his chair and was standing behind his desk, pointing an accusatory finger at Declan.

Declan was at a loss. What on the tape had made Henry lose it this way? Could he really be that bad that this guy was furious that Declan was wasting his precious time? Wouldn't his agent, Alan, or Rowdy have let him know if that was the case so he wouldn't be put in any embarrassing situations? Like this one.

This guy may be a tough critic, but Declan's audition tape wasn't that bad. It must be something else.

Declan eased his way toward the desk, not wanting to make any sudden moves, and lowered himself into one of the chairs that faced Henry. "Henry, sit down and tell me what this is all about. I'm not making any sense of this."

"I'll have you know my ten-year-old grandson watched that tape. Or the first thirty seconds of it until I could find the remote and shut the filth off." Henry sat, calming just a fraction, but his face was still beet red.

"What filth? You thought my audition tape was filth?" As Declan said it, he got just a hint of a tremor in his gut. The kind he felt when he'd thrown a touchdown pass but saw a ref throw a flag. It was the waiting to find out what was wrong than made him feel this way. He had an inkling of what might have made Henry label his audition tape filth, but he needed to wait to see what the ruling was.

"If that was an audition tape, then what the hell kind of job were you auditioning for? Gigolo?"

The tremor descended into full-fledged ache in his gut as

Declan, now sure what had happened, but hoping for a miracle, continued, "Henry, what exactly was on that DVD?"

Henry looked at Declan, his temper calming as he realized that maybe Declan was truly unaware of what had happened. He took the DVD from his desk drawer and threw it at Declan. "See for yourself." He motioned to the wall that held an elaborate entertainment center.

Declan got out of his chair, and, like the walk of a man on death row, made his way to the DVD player. He put in the disc and turned on the TV, but he knew what would be on the screen before he hit the button. He was right. It was he and Marlee, making love on the desk.

If it hadn't been for the surrounding circumstances, Declan would have pulled up a chair and watched his beautiful Marlee, but he rapidly hit the stop button and ejected the DVD. He carried it back to the chair and sat down. He could barely raise his head to make eye contact, but he did. "Henry, I don't know what to say. Obviously there's been a horrible mistake."

"Then you didn't purposely send me that tape?"

"Hell no."

Henry seemed to relax at that. "I hoped not. We've never met, Declan, but I'd like to think I'm a good judge of character and I was quite shocked when I received this and thought this was your idea of a joke."

"No, no. It was no joke. The courier took the wrong flash drive from my hotel room yesterday." The two men sat in silence, neither one knowing what to say. "Henry, you said your grandson saw this?"

"Yes. He and his parents were having dinner at my house last night. I had taken the DVD home to watch it there so I could be prepared when we met this morning. Aaron—that's my grandson—he's a big fan of yours so I let him watch it with me. Needless to say, we were both rather upset."

Declan hung his head, "Henry, I'm so sorry. It was never my intention for anyone to see this tape. Ever."

"I believe you, Declan, but next time you're going to tape yourself with some floozy, you better be more careful with the end result."

Even though he knew he had no grounds for outrage, Declan felt his temper rise. "She's no floozy, Henry. She's the woman I love."

"Be that as it may, we have no room for a man whose, shall we say, indiscretions could so easily fall into the hands of tabloid journalists. I'm sorry, Declan, but we're going to pass."

"Of course, Henry, I understand." Declan started to walk toward the door, the DVD in his hand, still in a state of shock.

"Declan?"

"Yes?" He turned to face Henry and was surprised to see a look of compassion on the older man's face.

"That DVD was only in my possession, and you have it back, but I'm assuming you sent the tape to the other networks as well…" He let the thought reach Declan.

"Oh my God." Declan ran to the door with the speed of the league's fastest running back while also reaching in his pocket for his phone.

He had called Alan on his cell as he'd left Henry Albright's office and, without going into too much detail, had Alan call all the execs he was to meet with and cancel. He needed to get those DVDs back personally, no trusting couriers or underlings for this, and he wouldn't be able to concentrate on selling himself to executives until he did.

Alan tried to talk him out of canceling. "You don't cancel

on these people, Declan. We've had these meetings set up for months. These next few weeks is when they're shoring up their personnel for next season, you need to be seen now."

"Alan, it's not going to happen. I have to get those tapes back, and then I have to go see Marlee."

"Again with this Marlee person. Would you just get her out of your system so we can concentrate on business?"

"That's not going to happen either. Just make the calls, Alan, and I'll call you when I've got the tapes back."

After three days of nonstop running all over New York City and Connecticut, Declan had all the DVDs back in his possession. He he'd gone to each network after he left Henry Albright, trying to track the things down. He'd been lucky. Two of the network honchos hadn't even viewed it yet. They were still in the sealed courier pouch.

It was now Sunday afternoon and Declan was back in his hotel room in New York with all the DVDs. He destroyed them all but his original one, the one on the flash drive with the red X. He logically knew he should destroy that one too, but he couldn't bring himself to do it.

He had to talk to Marlee, and what he had to say needed to be said face to face. He had all the DVDs back, but he had no idea if there were any copies out there floating around. The DVD in Connecticut had taken several days to get his hands on—any tech or coffee boy could have made a copy of it and could be sending it off to some tabloid at this moment. Or posted it anywhere online.

He'd done a quick search to see if maybe anybody had posted it, but thankfully nothing turned up.

He needed to tell Marlee that it was a possibility. Remote, yes, but a possibility nonetheless. He would never forgive himself if Marlee saw footage of herself and Declan on TV or the internet before Declan could talk to her. She would think he did it with the tape she'd given him. With the note that said she trusted him.

He called her phone several times but she didn't pick up. He didn't want to leave a voicemail, but after the fourth try he finally did. Not about to tell her over the phone that there was a possibility their sex tape might end up online, Declan just asked her to call him as soon as she could.

Not knowing if she'd call him back, or if she'd even listen to his voicemail, he pulled out the copy he had made of Marlee's itinerary. She would be arriving in Gainesville tonight, with a lecture at the University of Florida tomorrow night. He called the hotel that was listed on her itinerary and was surprised to find that the reservation for Marlee Reeves had been canceled. Odd.

He called the hotel in Chapel Hill where she had stayed until this morning. They said she had checked out on Friday. That was even more odd. She was lecturing at North Carolina on Friday night and then had Saturday off which she was spending in Chapel Hill before flying to Gainesville on Sunday. Why would she check out of her hotel Friday morning?

Declan looked through Marlee's itinerary. On the back were names and phone numbers of the contacts she worked with at each university. He called the North Carolina number. It was for a man named Thornton Grant, and apparently he was high up in the Communications Department.

"Hello?"

"Hello, I'm trying to reach a Thornton Grant."

"This is Thornton Grant."

"Mr. Grant, I'm trying to reach Professor Marlee Reeves. She had you down as a contact for —"

"I have no contact whatsoever with Ms. Reeves from this

point on." His voice had an uppity quality to it that put Declan on alert.

"But did you see Ms. Reeves on Friday? Did you see her when she lectured at your university?"

"Ms. Reeves did not lecture here on Friday. We, at the University of North Carolina, have very high moral standards attached with those that we invite to speak at our university, and Ms. Reeves is not among those who qualify."

Oh, God. The dread that rushed through Declan was palpable. The tape had gotten out. But where? He had grabbed every paper he could find, every tabloid, had been on the internet till two in the morning hitting every site that came up in a search for Declan Tate, and he had seen nothing to indicate a copy of the tape had been made.

"Mr. Grant, I don't understand. Professor Reeves was scheduled to lecture there Friday night."

"Scheduled and canceled."

"She canceled her lecture?" Something must really be wrong if Marlee canceled. She must have been dying of shame and couldn't face the public. Declan's heart broke to think of him causing Marlee pain.

"*She* did not cancel. *I* canceled *her*. And I don't mind saying I made some phone calls to my colleagues at other universities with the recommendation that they do the same." He had a sick sense of pride behind his voice, like he had single-handedly saved academia from the evil that was Marlee Reeves. Declan wanted to reach through the phone line and throttle the guy.

"But she lectured at Duke on Thursday?"

"She did, and I happened to be in attendance. Let us say, she never made it past her opening remarks." Grant paused; he seemed to be reveling in the memory of Marlee's apparent debacle. Then, as if realizing he had no idea who he was speaking to, he added, "Is this a journalist?"

"No. My name is Declan Tate. I'm a friend of Professor Reeves and I'm trying to get in touch with her."

"Aahh, Mr. Tate. The possible co-star in Ms. Reeves' brilliant acting debut?"

Declan had his answer. The tape was definitely out. He had to talk to Marlee. Now.

"Mr. Grant, do you have any idea where Marlee is?"

"I suspect she has gone back to Boston College with her tail between her legs."

Declan hung up the phone and started to pack his bags.

Chapter 20

Marlee threw her pen down on her desk, unable to concentrate. It was Wednesday afternoon and she was in her office on campus waiting to hear her fate. She didn't think she'd be fired, but she couldn't be sure. It all seemed surreal, as if it were some B-movie, not her life.

She had woken up last Thursday morning with Declan's scarf still wrapped around her in a hotel room in North Carolina. That was the last clear memory she had. The rest was a blur.

Spending the day in her room, feeling blue about Declan. Getting dressed. Putting her laptop, the flash drive with her presentation and video she opened her lecture with, and her notes into her satchel. Arriving at the auditorium. Reaching into the satchel and giving the facility manager the drive, which he would take to the control booth, and her notes, which he would place on the podium for her. He gave her the remote that would allow her to move the PowerPoint presentation along as she spoke.

Waiting backstage. Feeling a few tiny butterflies of nerves even though she was an expert at public speaking. The house

222 • MARA JACOBS

lights going down. Marlee stepping to the podium on the darkened stage, where a spotlight would appear on her when the video was over. The tape beginning. A hush like she had never heard falling over the crowd. Her turning to see which image on the video had that kind of effect on the crowd. Her audible gasp as she saw the images, twenty feet high, of her and Declan having sex on a desk. The kid in the booth, transfixed by the images, letting the video play, even though she was motioning wildly for him to cut it and clicking the remote furiously. But the remote was for the PowerPoint, not the video.

It seemed to go on forever, until the kid finally cut the feed to the large screen behind her. It had probably only been twenty or thirty seconds, but it had felt like twenty minutes. Professor Epley came onstage and took her by the arm and led her off. She was too stunned to move.

Marlee was shaken and was led to a soft couch backstage. Professor Epley, a paternal sort, knew that some kind of awful mistake had been made and was very understanding. He ran to the booth and got the flash drive back from the student there and handed it to Marlee. She was grasping in her satchel, coming up with the correct drive, as if that was explanation enough.

There was no way Marlee could face that crowd now. The lecture would be canceled; it was a mutual agreement. There was an announcement made to the audience and the lights went up as the crowd slowly streamed from their seats. The students in the crowd got a little unruly, yelling snarky comments out. Thanks goodness she couldn't make out what they were saying from where she was sitting.

And also thank God that mostly Declan's back had been to the camera during those first seconds of the tape. To her knowledge, no one had confirmed that the man bent over

Professor Marlee Reeves was NFL MVP Declan Tate. Though she thought she heard some whispering of Declan's name backstage.

And another saving grace was that it didn't appear that anybody had pulled out their cell phones and started filming the screen.

Thornton Grant, who was attending her lecture in advance, came backstage and made a scene. A very ugly scene. Words like "immoral" and "unethical" were bandied about, but Marlee could only sit on the couch, clutching the two flash drives—the one that had played, and the one that was supposed to have played.

Professor Epley got her back to her hotel. She waited there until she got the call from the dean of Boston College's Communications Department telling her to come home, that the entire series had been canceled, thanks mostly to Thornton Grant.

Now the dean was meeting with several of Marlee's peers from the department to decide what should be done.

The shock of the incident had worn off by now, and there was only anger at herself for being so careless with the drives. It was this anger that had fueled Marlee the past three days as she explained to the committee what had happened, and now waited. And waited. They expected to have some sort of answer for her today, so Marlee was stationed in her office.

As if someone sensed she was about to burst if she didn't get some answers, there was a knock on her door. Robert Curtis came in and sat down in front of Marlee.

"Robert, you're the messenger?" It was sort of appropriate. The only person other than her family that had seen Declan and her together was the one bringing her the outcome.

"Yes. The dean was going to call you in, but I asked if I could talk to you alone instead."

224 • MARA JACOBS

"Thank you, Robert. I think."

He had a soft smile. "It's not so bad, Marlee. You're off the lecture series, permanently. Because you represent BC, it was best felt that you not lecture anymore on this topic. But all else remains the same. Because the semester doesn't start until next week, they're going to try to rush and get you a few classes to teach. If not, you will just have office hours this semester."

A sigh of obvious relief escaped Marlee. She would miss being able to crusade on behalf of bringing awareness to the decline of public speaking, but was elated that she'd still be able to teach.

Robert got up to leave, then sat back down. "Marlee, I hope you don't mind me asking, are you and Declan serious?"

She looked down at her hands clasped together on her desk. How did she answer that? Did the fact that she loved Declan more than she ever thought possible mean it was serious? "No, Robert. It was just a…fling, I guess you'd call it."

Robert seemed taken aback. No one that knew Marlee very well thought of her as the fling type. "I hope it was worth it, Marlee. You're little fling with Declan cost you a lot of respect amongst your peers, and the chance to make a name for yourself in the academic world." He got up and left, giving Marlee's hands a comforting pat as he left. He didn't even hear her as she answered him in a soft whisper.

"It cost me more than that."

It had cost her her heart.

THREE WEEKS INTO THE NEW SEMESTER, MARLEE WAS able to get through the day of classes with her mind turning to Declan only five or six times. She considered that a marked improvement.

The department was able to squeeze a full load of classes for her to teach, and she was grateful to have the diversion. They were all classes she had taught many times before, so she had all the prep work done.

She was eternally grateful that the reason for the canceled lecture series never became public knowledge. Only a few people at Boston College knew, or cared, and they were peers of Marlee's and so kept their mouths shut.

Kathy had commiserated with Marlee over her loss on the phone while they both drank margaritas. It had taken all her willpower not to call Declan that night after she came home from work, so she'd called her friend instead.

After she hung up with Kathy, a drunken Marlee rationalized that she just wanted to see how Declan was doing. If he had wowed the networks? If he had accepted a position? If he was already living in New York? The truth of it was that Marlee just wanted to hear his voice. That sexy, husky Declan Tate voice.

In the end, she didn't call. Even through the tequila-induced haze she knew it was a bad idea. She wasn't even sure where he was.

She'd gotten several voicemails from him one day, and then nothing since. It'd been right after the Duke incident and Marlee had been too raw to return his calls. It occurred to her later that she should have given him a heads-up that he'd been a star at Duke for about twenty seconds.

Now Marlee replayed the night she'd gotten drunk on the phone with Kathy. It was so out of character for her, and she shivered as she remembered the day-long hangover she'd had the next morning. It would be a long time before she drank another margarita.

Her stomach turned from just thinking about the drink as she pulled into her garage after a full day. She grabbed her mail from the box and entered the kitchen. Not even her beloved kitchen gave her the same joy it did before Declan.

Was that how she would view life from now on? In measurements of before Declan and after Declan?

There was the usual junk mail, a few bills, and a package. She opened the package first and saw it was a flash drive. Trepidation rippled through Marlee. Oh, God. Not the tape. She turned it over and was not surprised to find a note taped to it, just like she had found before. Her hands trembled as she opened it.

Watch the tape, Marlee.

It's not the one you think it is.

The handwriting was Declan's. She was frozen in the kitchen. She slid her glasses up her nose and read the note again. And again. She slowly made her way to the den and connected the drive to her computer, and setting it so it would play on the TV. She took the remote with her to the recliner. At the last moment, she bypassed the recliner, thinking of another time, and another tape, and instead settled herself on the couch. She steeled herself and hit play.

It was the studio where she and Declan had worked. She almost hit the stop button, thinking it was the tape of her and Declan, but she waited. Something was a little different. And then Declan came into view, walking from behind where the camera was, to the set with the armchairs. The set only had one chair this time (that was what was different), and Declan went straight to it and sat down. The camera was zoomed in tight on Declan in the chair, only able to see his upper body and face.

That face. A feeling of loss ripped through Marlee. Even now, just seeing his face, she felt as though she'd been tackled. He hadn't changed—still the same drop-dead gorgeous Declan she knew. And loved.

Marlee watched intently as Declan hung his head, trying to compose himself, then looked straight into the camera and began speaking.

"Marlee, I tried like hell to get a hold of you those first few days after your Duke lecture."

So he did know about Duke. She was filled with shame. Here she had gotten on her high horse to him about trust and she'd let it be played to a room of two thousand. She was mortified, but Declan's voice brought her attention back to the screen.

"I didn't know what happened at first. I thought…" He seemed to struggle with his next words. "I thought my copy of the tape had gotten out and ruined your reputation."

Why would he think that? Then she listened as Declan explained what had happened to him in New York. She didn't know whether to be furious or laugh. How could she be furious when the same thing had happened to her? At least Declan had gotten the tapes back before anybody but a few network people had seen it.

"Anyway, after I got the tapes back I knew I had to let you know about it, in case somebody had made a copy of it or put it on the internet or some dumb-ass thing. You needed to be warned. But I couldn't find you. I called all around and finally this idiot Thornton something-or-other told me about Duke. I tried your landline at home but you didn't pick up, and I didn't want to say what I had to on voicemail."

Declan paused, taking a breath, his strong shoulders quaking, then looked at the camera again and went on. "I finally remembered Robert Curtis and got his number through Boston College information. By this time they'd had their meetings and he'd talked with you. He told me the whole story.

"I'm so sorry, Marlee, that all this happened. That the tape we made caused all of this. I told you I wanted to make the tape so you could see how beautiful you are to me, Marlee, and that's true. But there was another reason."

Again, Declan put his head down, this time clearing his throat and rubbing the back of his neck. Marlee got the feeling he was trying to get his courage up for the next part, and she felt a darkness fall over her. She couldn't imagine what he needed to say now? They were over, done. Did he really need to reiterate that on video? Did she really need to watch it?

She fingered the stop button on the remote, then took her finger off, letting the video play on. Declan, his green eyes shining, looked straight at her.

"I love you, Marlee. And I will always love you. I was hoping the tape would make you see that, and make you see that you love me too. That's why I wanted to make it."

On the couch, the remote fell from Marlee's hands as she raised them to her mouth, stunned by Declan's declaration.

"But somewhere along the line I realized that you could never love me. Not after what Justin did to you. You didn't seem able to see that not all ball players were the same." He spat that out with an exaggerated contempt, and Marlee felt shame rush through her. "And so the tape became something else to me. It was just a little piece of you that I could take with me. To have something of you forever, Marlee.

"It didn't work, though, having the tape. It's not enough. It will never be enough. I couldn't live with the thought that I never told you I love you, so, I'm telling you now. I love you, Marlee, and I want a future with you. And I don't want to wait until I have everything in my life figured out. Hell, that may never happen.

"I want to marry you, Professor Marlee Reeves, and have babies with you and Friday night dinners with your family and to cook with you every night in the kitchen…"

He took a deep breath, trying to compose himself, while Marlee waited, tears streaming down her face.

"I'm not sure which day you'll get this tape in the mail, probably Tuesday or Wednesday. I'll be at Gino's place every night this week waiting for you. If you can see yourself with me for the long haul, Marlee—and that means no dropping hands, no embarrassment over your husband's former profession—then meet me there. I'll be at our table, in the back, waiting. If I don't see you by Saturday night, I'll know the answer is no, and I'll just have to live with only seeing you on tape."

He paused. Marlee was sure it was for dramatic effect. Damn him—it was dramatic enough, just get on with it!

"The ball is in your possession, Marlee. It's first down, baby, and it's your play to call."

She could see the movement of his arm as he reached for the remote and then the screen went black.

She didn't even bother turning off the TV. She was already running through the house to the kitchen, where she gathered up her coat, keys, and purse, and then on to the garage.

And to Declan.

Epilogue

I n the end, they found they had a major issue on which they had totally opposing views.

The size of their wedding.

Marlee wanted something small, just close friends and family. Declan wanted to announce to the world that he was marrying Marlee.

One week after their tearful reunion at Gino's, with Gino himself crying the loudest as Declan got down on one knee and properly proposed to an accepting Marlee, the football coach at Boston College called Declan.

Boyd Parson and Declan had been teammates at Ohio State and had kept in touch over the years, especially once Declan had moved to Boston. Boyd offered Declan a position as offensive coordinator with Boston College. He was almost apologetic in his offering, assuming that someone of Declan's stature would never want to stoop as low as an assistant to a near-bottom-of-the-conference team.

Declan was ecstatic and, after discussing it with Marlee, quickly accepted Boyd's offer. It would still mean being on the road in the fall and during recruiting season, but it would put Declan back in the locker room, back on a team.

Marlee knew this was the right choice for Declan. He was already so happy to be going off to work every morning. And coming home to her every night.

"You know," Declan began one night as they lay side by side in bed, worn out from an especially exerting lovemaking session where Declan had tried to demonstrate to a very willing Marlee the advantages of a zone defense. "Those tapes falling into the wrong hands was the best thing that ever happened to us."

Remembering the humiliation she felt at Duke and the chastising from that windbag Thornton Grant, Marlee said, "I wouldn't go that far." But she chuckled. He was probably right.

Declan flipped her over to her back and began arousing her all over again, "Well, darlin'," he drawled. "Just how far would you go?"

Marlee, never able to get enough of Declan, proceeded to show him. "All the way to the end zone, darlin'."

Also By Mara Jacobs

Contemporary Romance ~ The Worth Series

Worth The Weight

Worth The Drive

Worth The Fall

Worth The Effort

Totally Worth Christmas

Worth The Price

Worth The Lies

Worth The Flight

Contemporary Romance ~ The Freshman Roommates Series

In Too Deep

In Too Fast

In Too Hard

Mystery ~ Anna Dawson's Vegas Series

Against The Odds

Against The Spread

Against The Rules

Against The Wall

Romantic Suspense

Broken Wings

Anthology

Countdown To A Kiss

Mara Jacobs is the New York Times and USA Today bestselling author of the Worth series.

After graduating from Michigan State University with a degree in advertising, Mara spent several years working at daily newspapers in advertising sales and production. This certainly prepared her for the world of deadlines!

She writes mysteries with romance, thrillers with romance, and romances with...well, you get it.

Forever a Yooper (someone who hails from Michigan's glorious Upper Peninsula), Mara now splits her time between the U.P. and Las Vegas.

Mara loves to hear from readers, contact her at:
www.marajacobs.com
mara@marajacobs.com

Made in United States
Orlando, FL
06 September 2023

36763950R00143